WILD WAVES
AND
WISHING WELLS

WILD WAVES
AND
WISHING WELLS

Irish Folk Tales for Children

Órla Mc Govern
Illustrated by Gala Tomasso

*This book is dedicated to The Blackrock Babes,
and all the sea swimmers around Ireland.*

*Special thanks to Niceol, Gala, Tara, Leigh,
Beka, Juley-Ann, and all my friends and
family who inspired me to tell stories.*

First published 2019

The History Press
The Mill, Brimscombe Port
Stroud, Gloucestershire, GL5 2QG
www.thehistorypress.co.uk

British Library Cataloguing in Publication Data.
A catalogue record for this book is available from the British Library.

ISBN 978 0 7509 9048 6

Typesetting and origination by The History Press
Printed and bound by TJ International Ltd.

CONTENTS

ABOUT THE AUTHOR AND ILLUSTRATOR

ÓRLA MC GOVERN is a writer, storyteller and performer. She grew up in Dublin, travelled around the world for a bit, and now lives (mostly) in Galway on the west coast of Ireland. She loves making things up – stories, songs, plays, sometimes just dinner! She is a committee member of Storytellers of Ireland, and this is her second book with The History Press; her first being *Dublin Folk Tales for Children*. Órla loves to swim in the sea.

GALA TOMASSO studied Art and Design in England, Fine Art at Burren College of Art in Clare, and Design at DIT Dublin. Originally from Scotland, she has had her roots in Galway for twenty-five years and currently lives in Connemara. Gala also illustrated *Dublin Folk Tales for Children*.

INTRODUCTION

Hello readers! You are very welcome to my book of Irish folk tales, called *Wild Waves and Wishing Wells*. This is your book now!

As the title suggests, this book has a lot of stories about water: the sea, wells, some lakes and rivers, and even perhaps a puddle! I love the water, and I love to swim in the sea near my home in Galway, so stories about water make me very happy.

This is a book of folk tales, and for me that means stories by folk and for folk. I'm folk and you're folk, so please enjoy it! Some of these stories are very old, stories I heard as a child, and I have written my version of them as I remember. Other stories I have heard just a bit of, and have had to fill in the missing parts, while some stories come from my imagination, after visiting a particular place that I thought was unusual or special.

It is great to read stories in a book, and it is also great to tell them out loud and see how much you remember. Telling stories out loud is called storytelling. Each time you

tell a story, it is a little different. It's a bit like the waves in the sea; sometimes the same story can be louder or quieter, a bit scarier or a bit more gentle, warm or cold. I love the way a good story is like the sea, moving and changing, drawing the listeners in. It feels different every time we experience it.

As you tell a story, you might forget a bit or add in a brand new bit. You might even stretch it out a bit longer if your audience is really enjoying it! If you practice telling stories, it's really nice to have a listener. They can become part of your story too, and join in with noises and words if you ask them.

You can practice your storytelling with the stories from this book. Once you read them, see which parts you remember the best, and tell them out loud to a friend. If you change the story a little, or make up brand new bits, it doesn't matter, it just means that wave has moved in a different direction!

I would love to hear new versions of these stories. Perhaps I'll be lucky and one or two will crash up on the shore one day!

I've put some notes at the back of the book for you – little facts you might find interesting, or words that you might like to learn more about.

I hope you enjoy reading these stories, saying them out loud, and splashing around with the words!

1

FIONN AND THE SALMON

What a special fish it was
That lived there in the Boyne,
And what a gift it did bestow
Worth more than golden coin.

Fionn Mac Cumhaill was a very famous character in Ireland long ago, and this is one story from his life.

When Fionn was a lad he was sent off, away from home, to study. It was a bit like going to a boarding school, except he was to be the only student there.

The person he was sent to study with was very wise indeed. His name was Finnegas, and he was a poet who wrote beautiful words about almost everything – and most of the time his poems rhymed!

Finnegas had been writing poems all his life, and everyone knew how good he was at it. But he was clever in other ways too. He had, in his brain, all sorts of information: old stories, knowledge of which plants to use as medicine when you were sick, and the names of all the stars and planets in the sky. He could tell you a lot about the animals in the woods, about the stones and mountains, and all about the kings and queens of Ireland, and of other countries too! Over all, he was a very smart person indeed.

Finnegas lived on the banks of the River Boyne, and by day, Fionn would help his teacher by cleaning, cooking, mending clothes, and doing other little jobs. When evening came, Fionn would sit by the fire, listening to all the great stories and ideas that came from the words of his teacher. Fionn soaked up all this knowledge like a sponge!

Now, remember how I told you how clever Finnegas was? Well, even though that was the case, Fionn was very curious and asked Finnegas an awful lot of questions. Most of them Finnegas had answers for, but even he couldn't answer every single question – no teacher could! Finnegas, however, wanted to be nothing less than the wisest human in the whole world, and he had a plan to do just that! The key to this was in an old prophecy.

It was said there was a sacred hazel tree that grew near the banks of the Boyne, and that this tree held all the knowledge of the world. But neither Finnegas nor anyone else knew where this tree was. Its location was a secret. What he did know, however, was that a certain salmon would swim to the bank beside the tree and eat the nuts that fell into the water. For sometimes knowledge is a very delicious thing!

'All I have to do,' he told Fionn, 'is catch that salmon, you see?' Fionn shook his head, puzzled.

'Oh Fionn,' said Finnegas. 'If all of the knowledge of the world is in that tree, then it is also in the hazelnuts; and if the salmon eats the nuts, then it is also in the salmon. Then if I catch the salmon …'

'Ah!' said Fionn. 'If you catch the salmon and eat it for your dinner, then you will possess all the knowledge of the world!'

'Exactly my boy!' said Finnegas. 'And you will help me catch it!'

And that was how it was for quite a while. Each day Fionn would spend a good amount of time helping Finnegas with his work around the house: cooking, cleaning, chopping wood, making the fires, and, of course, checking the fishing rod when Finnegas was not fishing himself.

In the evenings, Finnegas would be Fionn's teacher: reciting great poems and sagas, telling him the history of great kings and queens, and stories of the land.

One morning, Fionn woke from his bed by the fire to very loud noises. There was shouting, banging of pots and pans, and laughter. He rubbed his sleepy eyes, trying to figure it all out, and it was then that he realised all the noise was coming from Finnegas. The poet was laughing and whooping, throwing pots in the air, and shouting 'Yipppeeeeeeeee!'

When he saw Fionn he ran over and hugged the lad so tightly that Fionn thought his bones might break!

'We did it! We did it! We did it!' Finnegas cried, pulling Fionn into a little dance with him. 'Well, I did it actually!'

'Did what, Finnegas?' asked Fionn, still half asleep.

'Oh you silly lad,' said Finnegas, 'I did **IT**. There's only one **IT** that matters. I caught the Salmon of Knowledge!'

Fionn's eyes widened, and he grinned a big grin. 'Oh, that's such great news!' he beamed.

'I couldn't have done it without you, lad,' said Finnegas. 'You helped me set that fishing rod only last night. Good work my boy, you will be rewarded,' and he shook Fionn's hand. 'Now, we must set to work. Time is ticking. That salmon is fresh but it won't stay that way for ever.'

Finnegas instructed Fionn to build a cooking fire. A good steady one with flat logs underneath, so the cooking pan would sit on them perfectly. Finnegas then gently placed the fish on the pan and covered it.

'I'm going to head off to the woods to pick some herbs as a garnish,' he said. 'I'm sure that salmon will be magical when I eat it, but I also want it to be delicious! You are in charge of the cooking, Fionn.' Fionn smiled and nodded.

Finnegas picked up the basket to collect the herbs, then turned back, with a very serious look on his face.

'That is my salmon in the pan. Under **NO** circumstances are you to eat any before I get back, do you understand?' Fionn nodded nervously, as Finnegas continued.

'It is **MY** salmon, and it is **MY** knowledge, Fionn. Once I have taken the first bite, all the knowledge of the fish will go into me.' His serious face disappeared then and turned into a smile. 'Then I will happily share my meal with you, my young friend!'

And with that off Finegas ran into the woods, singing with pure happiness as he went: 'I caught the magic salmon, I caught the magic salmon, soon I'll be the wiiiisest one of any in this worrrrrld!'

Fionn set about setting the table for dinner. He was so happy for his teacher and wanted everything to be perfect for when he returned. As Fionn had his back turned to the fire, the wind picked up and fanned the flames. The salmon hissed and crackled in the pan.

'Oh no!' thought Fionn, 'I can't let it burn!' And without thinking, he poked at the skin of the salmon to see if it was all right. As he did so, he let out a roar – the hot fish burned his thumb! He immediately stuck his thumb into his mouth to ease the pain.

A few minutes later, Finnegas returned with his basket full of herbs. He saw the beautiful table, all laid out for dinner, and in the middle was the Salmon of Knowledge, ready to be eaten. But as he sat down at the table, he noticed something unusual about

Fionn: it was as if there was a strange light shining from his eyes.

'Have you eaten a piece of my salmon?' he asked Fionn.

'No, teacher,' Fionn replied.

'Have you chewed a bit of the skin while it was cooking?'

'No, teacher.'

'Have you drank of the juices that dripped from the fish?'

'No, teacher,' said Fionn. 'But …'

Fionn hesitated, then he told Finnegas how he had burned his thumb, had put it in his mouth to ease the pain, and for just one second had tasted the fish.

Finnegas bowed his head. 'Well, my boy, all the wisdom of the world is now yours. You were the first to taste the Salmon of Knowledge, even if it was by accident.'

He instructed Fionn to eat the fish, as it was now his to claim. After the fish was eaten, Fionn told Finnegas that he didn't really feel that different. He didn't feel any wiser than before.

'You first tasted the fish with your thumb, so suck your thumb again,' said Finnegas.

Fionn did so, and in that moment all the knowledge of the world rushed into his head in one go!

Finnegas said goodbye to Fionn, shook his hand, and sent him on his way that very night, for there was no more that he could teach him. He knew that Fionn was destined to be a great poet, warrior, and leader when he grew up. He was happy that he had at least helped Fionn on his path to greatness.

When Fionn left, Finnegas sat down by the fire, and let out a big sigh.

'Well, I suppose it's sandwiches again for dinner tonight!'

2

THE BOY WHO BECAME A LAKE

Long ago, in the rolling hills of Clare, there lived a young lad named Turlough. He had sparkling eyes, thick curly hair, and a good sprinkling of mischief! Some might say too much mischief.

'That lad is up to his tricks again!'

'What is he up to now?'

'Turlough! It must have been Turlough!'

Those were the types of things you would hear people say in Turlough's village when he walked down the street.

I have to tell you, yes, it is true, Turlough was very fond of all sorts of jokes, and yes, he often caused quite a bit of mischief. For example:

You would wake up and find all your cows in the field were wearing daisy chains!

You would go to gather the milk from the pail and find he had replaced it with apple juice!

You would go to put on your shoes and find them full of mushrooms!

Now, these little jokes were not that bad really; in fact, they often sparked a lot of laughter, so much so that Turlough was favoured by the fairy folk (who were fond of a joke themselves!). They often found themselves laughing at Turlough's antics, so he always remained in their good books. They knew that he had a good heart and all he wanted in life was a bit of fun.

But sometimes Turlough's jokes went a bit too far for some people. Powerful people.

And one night, Turlough went too far with none other than Allód, the great king of the sea. Allód was grumpy at the best of times, never mind when a joke was played on him.

This could not end well.

This particular night, Turlough was up to the usual mischief by the seashore. He was whistling tunes and skimming stones on the water, when didn't he spot Allód, king of the sea, sleeping down beneath the waves in his sea bed.

'Look at him sleeping, snoring away,' giggled Turlough. 'I'll soon fix that!' And he slipped down beneath the waves to make a big pile of mischief below.

He watched the king, fast asleep on his bed. The king's long black hair was spread out across a pillow of seaweed growing from a rock. Turlough swam up very quietly behind the king, and began to knot his hair and the seaweed together! Once they were well and truly knotted, he swam back up to the surface, picked up two big rocks and banged them together just under the water.

Bang, bang, bang.

Of course, the sound got louder and louder as it moved down through the water.

Bang, bang, BANG.

Until finally it reached King Allód, and woke him suddenly from his deep sleep, just like a big rocky alarm clock!

BANG, BANG, BANG!

King Allód leapt to his feet – or at least he tried to! His long hair was woven into the seaweed on the rock, and no sooner did he try to stand up than his hair tugged him back down again!

Turlough giggled from the shallow shore and watched as the great king landed smack on his bottom!

Again Allód tried to get up, but to no avail.

More giggles from Turlough.

The third time the king tried to stand, he was so angry that he pulled with great force, and this time some of his hair ripped out from the roots.

'OUCH!' cried the king. 'OUUUUUCH!'

Turlough stopped laughing. He didn't realise it would hurt that much!

The king was furious. He grabbed a razor shell and sliced away the remaining seaweed that was tied to his hair. His face was red, and he stomped around the seabed. Not only was he woken from his sleep, but his head was stinging. Not only was his head stinging, but he had lost a big chunk of his lovely hair. He was very fond of his hair.

'WHO DID THIS?' roared King Allód.

Turlough began to feel afraid.

'WHO DID THIS? THEY WILL SURELY PAY!'

Now Turlough was really afraid. It was time for him to get out of there before the king saw him.

But it was too late – the king had spotted him standing at the shore!

Turlough scrambled for safety away from the water, but heard a thundering voice behind him.

'Turlough!' shouted the king. 'I see you running away! Wait until I catch you!'

But there was NO WAY Turlough was waiting until the king caught him. He might have been a trickster, but he wasn't stupid!

Now, the king was fast and very powerful, but his feet had become tangled in the loose seaweed, causing him to trip and stumble on the rocks. This made him even angrier – **'TURLOUGH!!'** – but it did give Turlough a bit of extra time to escape from the sea.

Down Turlough ran along the beach, his heart pounding in his chest. Up Turlough scrambled along the sea cliffs, and as he did, he glanced back and saw the great sea king Allód rise up from the waves in pursuit.

'I will turn you into sea mist,' roared the king, 'and you will be blown to the four winds and trouble me no more!'

Turlough was terrified as he raced up the hills towards the Burren Forests. He knew if he could get far enough inland, then the king's power would fade the further he was from the sea. But it was of no use, his angry chaser was gaining on him!

'May you be turned to water …' cried Allód. He raised his mighty arms and he cast a spell – a curse – across the hills towards Turlough, '… and may the water be raised into sea mist and may you vanish into a hundred thousand drops and be blown into nothing!'

It was too late. The spell reached Turlough, and he felt a strange melting in his body.

'Quick, come down here!' said a voice.

Turlough turned to see some of his fairy friends appear and grab his arm. They led him through a grove and past a fairy mound. All the while, Turlough could feel his body begin to turn into water, his curls falling to the ground as little droplets: splash, splash, splash.

The fairies laid him down in the middle of the earth, and stood around him; but alas, they were too late to stop Turlogh becoming water, and they watched as he melted into a giant lake in front them.

'We must do something!' said one.

So the fairies circled Turlough and wove their own spell. They cast their magical words into the water. The sea mist stopped rising. Instead, the water simply stayed in the ground in the form of a lake.

When King Allód saw the lake appear, he was happy enough that some justice had been done, and that annoying lad would

never trouble anyone again. So he turned back to return to his home under the sea, rubbing his sore head.

But what of poor Turlough? No longer was he a boy full of laughter and mischief. Now all that was left of him was a lake on the side of the mountain.

Well, let me tell you this. There is always more to fairy magic than you think! Yes, it was true the boy had been turned into a lake, but the fairy spell gave him a little extra gift.

Several times a year, the fairies would draw the lake down with them below, into the fairy realm. Of course, they would always make sure that King Allód was nowhere to be seen. As he moved between the realms, Turlough would regain his human form. During this special time, he would once more be able to laugh and joke, and even get up to a little bit of mischief with his fairy friends!

Many, many years later, a young monk (who is now a saint) called Cronán was passing a certain spot on the mountain. He happened to glimpse over at the precise moment when Turlough changed! He witnessed the lake transforming into a human. He watched as feet, legs, torso, arms, head – and a big mop of curly hair formed from the tiny droplets. He watched the lake become a boy! Cronán thought it to be a miracle, and so he built a church on that spot, in honour of the mystical experience he had witnessed.

To this very day, it is said that Turlough still lives there, high in the Burren. It is also said that if he takes a fancy, he moves around to other places in Ireland. You can't always see him, because he disappears underground for a time to be with his fairy friends, perhaps playing a trick or two.

Not everyone may know of him, but his name is still remembered. In fact, it is often given to the bodies of water like this.

Turlough – the disappearing lake.

3

WELL, WELL, WELL

Dotted around the whole of Ireland are places and things that people call 'holy wells'. Some people might also call them 'sacred wells', 'magic wells' or 'fairy wells'.

These are places where water comes (or used to come) up from the ground into a well. Some of these places are as old as Ireland itself, and others are places that were dug and made by humans.

When the monks came to Ireland, they brought with them their Christian beliefs. They named new wells, but also changed the names of many of the old wells they

found, and called them after their holy
saints. Because of this, in Ireland you will
often have a well with two different names
(maybe more) and perhaps more than one
story attached to it.

The stories of the ancient pagan gods
of Ireland were quite different to what the
monks were used to. The old stories were
still told alongside the new ones, so, as a

result, over time many stories got blurred together and it became hard to tell what the very first story had been. This is not unusual with old stories.

A good example of this is if you come across a well called Brigit's well.

Brigit is the name of a goddess in the old pagan tradition, and St Bridget is the name of a saint in the Christian tradition. So when you hear a story about Brigit/Bridget, it could refer to either, or both – and well, it's hard to know which is which! Sometimes it doesn't matter at all, once it is a good story!

In the Irish language there are often different names for many of these places. Sometimes, the name of a place might be quite different in the English language as opposed to *as Gaeilge* (in the Irish language).

Figuring out the translation of the Irish place name may give you a clue to a whole different story you can ask about!

4

SON OF THE SEA

Manannán Mac Lir was a cool character with a cool name. He had many cool names: Manann, Oribsu (where the River Corrib got its name), and 'Lord of the Sea' (although his friends teased him a bit for that one).

His personal favourite was 'Son of the Sea'. Other people knew him as the 'Master of Tricks and Illusions'. He liked that one too (even though it was a bit long). He liked the idea of being a magician.

'Isn't it great,' thought Manannán, 'that I have all this great stuff that helps me live up to my magical names?'

It was true!

He had a beautiful horse called Enbarr, and, like many magical horses, Enbarr could travel over both land and sea. There was no need to climb down from the saddle and climb into a boat. Oh no, Enbarr was an

all-in-one-go type of horse. Enbarr had style. Enbarr had grace. Enbarr had the most beautiful long flowing mane, and always looked like he had just had a shampoo and blow-dry at the hairdressers.

Manannán was also a great man for the style and was himself a very snappy dresser. His clothes weren't just fashionable; they were also practical, by way of being magical. A good magician needs magical clothes!

He would often put on his very favourite coat when he went out with his pals for the night. His coat had a name all to itself. It was called 'The Cloak of Mists'. This coat was nothing like your average jacket. It was amazing! It could change to any colour or shade with one wish from Manannán.

He had lots of fun with this coat (as well as using it for more serious stuff). For example, Manannán would stand in front of a tree and shout 'Boo!' – then he would quickly pull his cloak around him and it would change colour to match the tree behind him!

'Who's there?' his friends would ask, puzzled. And Manannán would giggle to himself under his cloak. I suppose it was like an early model 'cloak of invisibility', because it could make you blend in just about anywhere, and seem to disappear.

As I mentioned, some of his cool stuff was used for more serious situations, like a battle. Like the sword he kept in his wardrobe. It was called Fragarach (which means 'The Answerer' in Irish). It was scary. If you were on the wrong side of it in battle, you wouldn't be able to answer very much at the end!

Even in the midst of a battle, Manannán was all about style. He had a powerful spear, sharp as any, but also painted beautifully in yellow and red. With that he had a matching magical shield that no weapon could pass through, no matter how hard his enemies tried (now that is a VERY handy thing to have in a battle).

Of all the cool things Manannán Mac Lir had though, my favourite would be

'Scuabtuinne' or 'The Wave Sweeper'. This was the name given to a very special boat. It needed no sails, no oars, and no engine! Not only was it automatic in days when there were no automatic boats, but it could also read the mind of its owner and go wherever their thoughts wanted. You just had to think of a place and it would 'sweep' you across the waves!

Cool!

Now, why would Manannán need a magical boat if he had a magical horse? Good question. Well, the boat could carry more people, if you were having a party or something, and he always needed a back-up plan for the days when Enbarr was busy washing his mane or at the hairdressers!

5

TIN WHISTLE SOUP

Mamie Reilly had a twitch. Now it wasn't a twitch in her hand or her face or her eye, it was a twitch in her curtain – for she was quite nosey you see!

She was always twitching her curtain, peeping out to see if something was happening so she could give out about it. Most of the time, nothing much was happening outside her window, but she was suspicious nonetheless.

'Did you see that?' she would say to her goldfish.

The goldfish was the only living thing she came close to liking, and that was mainly because the goldfish didn't speak.

'Did you see that?' she whispered. 'The neighbour's dog has taken a wee on my hedge, the dirty thing. The cheek of it!'

Now beside Mamie Reilly's cottage was a well. It was on the side of the road, so occasionally a stranger would stop on their travels for a drink of water.

'They'd better move right along,' said Mamie. 'They won't get anything at my house!'

The highlight of Mamie's day was when something happened that she could give out about.

'That good for nothing made a mess,' complained Mamie when a passer-by dropped his handkerchief by the well (by accident, of course).

Because people knew Mamie was grumpy, they avoided her as much as possible, so Mamie had no friends. This was a pity, because as well as being grumpy, she was lonely. In fact, her loneliness made her even grumpier.

Now this particular morning when Mamie woke up, she had no idea what a super-extra-highlight of a day she was about to have! As she was twitching at her curtain, she spotted a figure walking up the road towards the well.

'Move along!' she whispered.

The figure got closer and eventually reached the well.

'Move along!' she hissed.

But do you know what? The figure did not move along! It was a man with a bag on his back, and he stopped right between the well and Mamie's cottage. This man was a travelling musician.

Mamie knew he was a travelling musician by the clothes he wore, and the way his hair fell, and the way he hummed a little song to himself. She had seen his type before. They always wanted money or food in return, for what?

'In return for a few screechy tunes,' she muttered. 'Well, he won't get any money from me!'

The man took the bag off his back and began to unpack it on the ground. The amount of things coming out of it seemed a lot more than should have been able to fit into a bag that size! He took out a cooking pot and began to build a small fire at the side of the road.

Mamie was so annoyed! She opened the window and roared out, 'Don't be thinking you can set up camp here young man, there'll be no stopping the night outside my house!'

The man smiled back at her and waved. 'Don't worry, Missus, I won't stop the night where I am not invited. I will just cook my dinner and be on my way.'

'Hmph,' said Mamie, and she slammed the window shut.

That didn't stop her peeping though, and she twitched the curtains as she watched him build a fire and draw water from the well and put it in a pot.

The musician took out a small tin whistle from his bag and began to polish it very carefully, holding it up to the light, examining each end. The tin whistle glistened in the sunlight, and by now the people passing by were watching this display with some interest.

Who was this man?

What was he up to?

He placed his cooking pot on the fire, tied a piece of string to the tin whistle, and very carefully lowered it in.

'What are you making?' asked one man called Frank, who was watching from the road.

'Ah,' said the musician, 'I am brewing up tin whistle soup.'

'Tin whistle soup? What kind of a thing is that?' asked Frank, rubbing his beard with great curiosity. 'I've never tasted such a thing, is it nice?'

'It is delicious!' said the musician. 'And not only that, it the most magical soup ever invented!'

'What kind of magic?' asked Frank.

'If you drink a cup of it, you will find your heart filled with happiness and music,' said the musician.

'Hmm,' pondered Frank, 'how much do you want for a cup of it so?'

'Oh! This soup is not for sale!' said the musician. 'It is far too precious.'

Now Frank was surprised at this answer. He thought for sure that the musician was trying to sell something, so he started to walk away, his head down in disappointment.

'BUT,' said the musician, 'if you were to throw in a garnish for the soup, I'd be glad to share it with you. The soup is almost perfect as is, but it is the tradition to share it with all who add a garnish.'.

'A garnish?' said Frank.

'Yes, anything will do,' said the musician, 'a pinch of herbs, a vegetable, a ham bone …'

'I've these fresh carrots from my garden,' said Frank. 'I will throw them in.'

'Perfect,' said the musician, and they threw in the big juicy carrots.

The musician stirred the pot and tasted again. 'Mmm,' he said, and his voice was a little more musical. 'It's not quite ready yet though, the tin whistle needs to soak a little more.'

Then a lady, Mrs O'Brien, spoke up. 'I'd love to try it too. Can I add something?'

'Hmm,' said the musician, 'it is quite delicious as it is, but if you were to throw in a garnish, it is the tradition that I should share a cup with you too.'

'I've a big bag of spuds in my pantry, I will gladly throw them in!' she said.

'Perfect,' said the musician, and they threw in the big bag of pink potatoes.

A third person chimed in from the back of the crowd. 'Can I try it too, I've some lentils?'

'It would be rude of me to refuse the garnish,' said the musician, 'go ahead.'

The lentils were thrown in, and the musician tasted the soup.

'A little longer,' he said.

Then more and more people came forward wanting to try, offering various garnishes of stewing meat, spinach, vegetables, and herbs. The pot became so full that the soup had to be carefully transferred to a bigger pot to feed everyone.

At this point a huge crowd had gathered, and people were sharing their garnishes with those who had none to throw in, to make sure the whole village could try it.

The musician tasted it again. 'It is almost there,' he said, 'but it is missing a sprig of the finest rosemary.'

Everyone looked around. Did anyone have some? No?

The musician sniffed the air, then pointed over to Mamie's garden. 'There! There is the sweetest rosemary that I have ever smelled!'

The whole village turned towards Mamie's cottage. Her curtain stopped twitching. Everyone waited. Her front door creaked open, and Mamie poked her head out. She had never seen so many people looking at her at once. She scowled at them, but the musician was quick to charm her.

'Dear lady,' he said, 'in all my travels I have never smelled rosemary as sweet as this. If you place a sprig of it in the pot, I am sure the music I play will be the sweetest in all the land, to match the owner of the garnish!'

Mamie was taken aback; she'd never had someone compliment her before and didn't know what to say. All eyes were on her, as everyone was waiting for their soup.

She had to say something.

She looked down and at her side she saw a little boy, Seamus, looking up at her, a cup in his hand, and his eyes full of hope. Waiting.

'Well, if I will get a cup of soup out of it, I suppose I can spare a little sprig,' she said.

The crowd let out a big cheer.

'HOORAAAAY!'

The rosemary was picked and added to the soup.

The musician gave it a final stir and declared, 'It is ready!'

Carefully, he pulled out the tin whistle on the string, and rinsed it off.

He reached into the pot and served the first cup to Mamie. Everyone watched her again. As she sipped the soup the musician began to play a tune. Dee-di-de-diddle-de-di-de-dum, dee-di-de-diddle-de-di-de-dum. It was an old tune that Mamie's grandfather used to play, and before she could stop it, a tear came to her eye.

She finished the soup and gasped with satisfaction. 'That is the best soup I have tasted since I was a child!' For the first time in many years Mamie smiled.

The crowd cheered again, 'Hooray!' And the music started up. Fiddles and drums came from houses and the soup was served to the whole village as they sang and played and chatted. Everyone agreed it was a magical soup.

The mayor of the village had never seen anything like it, all these people, dancing, happy, and chatting away to each other. Even Mamie Reilly had thrown off her shoes and was dancing a jig to Frank's fiddle playing. The mayor had an idea.

'Will you sell that tin whistle to our village?' he asked the musician (who was having a break with his feet up and a pint of ale in his hand). 'I have never seen the people so happy, it would mean so much to us, and I will give you a fair price.'

'Ah I can't,' said the musician, sipping on his ale, 'for there is none other like it in the world.'

'I'll give you five times what it is worth,' said the mayor, 'you can buy a fine fiddle instead.'

The musician shook his head.

'I'll give you ten times what it's worth – you can buy a fine guitar that sings like an angel.'

The musician shook his head.

'I'll give you twenty times its worth,' said the mayor, 'you can buy a silver flute and live like a lord for the month of May.'

The musician rubbed his chin. 'Its value is priceless, but you have convinced me that you need it. Very well, I will accept your token, and must be on my way.'

The mayor was delighted. 'Every Saturday we will make tin whistle soup,' he announced, 'we'll keep the magical whistle in Mamie Reilly's house, near the well, and the whole town will be all the richer for these celebrations.'

Mamie beamed the biggest smile she had ever beamed. Her curtains would no longer be twitching because her door would always be open to her neighbours.

The mayor turned to the musician. 'And for your kindness, you will always have a bed and a place at the table in our town, whenever you are passing through.'

The musician thanked the mayor, packed his cooking pot in his bag and set it down, ready to go. Before he left, everyone wanted to shake his hand, so he made his way around, shaking hands and hugging the villagers.

Now the young boy, Seamus, happened to be standing close to this bag. When the musician set it down Seamus noticed there was a strange clinking sound. Like something else metal banging against the cooking pot. When nobody was looking, Seamus lifted the flap of the bag and peeped inside.

There, tied in a bundle, were twenty tin whistles, identical to the magical one that had made the soup!

Seamus gasped. Behind him stood the musician. He reached down and grabbed his bag. He put his finger to his lips and made a 'shhh' gesture to Seamus. He threw him a knowing wink, slung his bag over his shoulder, and walked out of the village and over the hill, humming a tune as he went.

Seamus was shocked. Did he know a secret nobody else knew?

All that night Seamus thought long and hard about the day's events for he was a deep-thinking young lad. When he had thought long enough, he smiled.

He knew that the travelling musician would go on to another town, set up his pot and his fire, and tell the story again. He knew that people would gather and become curious. He knew that people would offer little bits and pieces to throw into the pot so they could have a taste of the magical soup. He knew that the more 'little garnishes' people threw in, the better the soup would taste. He knew that in another town someone would want to buy the magical whistle, and after much bargaining, the musician would reluctantly sell it, for twenty times the price of a normal tin whistle!

But you know what else Seamus thought? Perhaps the musician had not lied.

Were it not for the whistle, the people in the village would not have not come together to cook their delicious soup.

Were it not for that whistle, they would not have gathered together to sing songs and dance.

Were it not for that whistle, Mamie Reilly would still be scowling and hiding behind her twitching curtains.

Were it not for that whistle, she would not have children knocking at her door on Saturdays, asking if they could see it, and neighbours stopping by for tea and biscuits, asking to play a tune.

Now, whenever a travelling person came by, the town would welcome them.

The whole village would take out the whistle and make a big pot of tin whistle soup together and sing and dance by the well.

No, there was no lie.

It really was a magic whistle.

6

WHAT A BIG BABY

You've already heard one story in this book about the great Irish hero, Fionn Mac Cumhaill. Well now, I've another one for you. This particular story took place later on in his life, when Fionn was older, and he lived in a house with his wife Úna and their little boy.

Of course, Fionn still had all the wisdom of the world, and he was also brave and very strong. The people of Ireland thought so much of him that they called him 'A Giant of a Man'.

Now it's true that Fionn was taller and stronger than most, but he wasn't really an actual giant (well, not quite as big as the kind we think of anyway). But words have wings, and wouldn't you know it, news of this Irish 'giant' travelled across the water to Scotland, where it reached the (very big) ears of Benandonner.

Now Benandonner was indeed a giant. As in he was HUGE.

'Who is this other giant fella?' he said, while drinking his huge cup of tea with his huge giant hands. 'Who is this Irish fella calling himself a giant? I am the giantest giant around these islands, and if anyone says different I will challenge them to a duel!' (That's a sort of fight.)

So, the word went out that Benandonner wanted to fight Fionn, and the word got louder and travelled across the water to Ireland. Now Fionn was no coward, so when he heard this he accepted the challenge right away.

'No man is too big for me to fight!' declared Fionn. 'In fact, I will make it easier for the two of us to meet.' And he set about building a bridge across to Scotland.

Of course, this was one way for Fionn to show his strength.

His wife Úna smiled. 'Fionn, everyone knows you are strong. Let you build just one half of the bridge, and let Benandonner build the other half. That is only fair as a start to a fight, and that way you'll be home for your dinner, and the pie I made for you won't be spoiled.'

'Very well,' said Fionn. 'Fair is fair.'

Fionn was strong and brave, but he was also smart enough to know that this made sense. And he didn't want to miss the lovely pie for his dinner!

He set about building the bridge. He wanted to make it strong so the fight would be on solid ground. He studied the way the bees made their beehives so sturdy, and copied their design, then he sculpted great columns of rock and placed them halfway across the water to Scotland. The fight was to take place the following week, but for now, Fionn was headed home.

'No man is too big for me to fight,' he said again.

But do you know what? That wasn't quite true.

For the very next week, Fionn got a delivery from his cousin in Scotland in the post. It was a giant wooden crate. On the outside was attached a note which began 'Fionn – you have to see this!'

'Dear Cousin,' continued the note, 'I am sending you this as a warning. Inside this crate is a boot I stole from outside the door of Benandonner's house. This is his BOOT for goodness' sake! If the foot of this man is this big, you can only imagine how big his whole self is. If you are going to fight him, all I can say is beware and good luck!'

Fionn pried open the crate with his axe, and inside was the biggest boot he had ever seen!

Fionn gulped, 'GULP.'

The boot was massive. It frightened Fionn so much so that he didn't want to look at it outside his house, so he pushed it over the cliff onto the beach below. It was so big that a little old widow saw it land on the beach and decided to move into it and live in it. She brought her cat and her chair with her, and still had room to stretch her legs.

Now poor Fionn was really worried.

His wife Úna saw him worrying and brought him a big cup of tea and a piece of soda cake to cheer him up.

'Fionn, my love,' said she, rubbing his worried head, 'of course you are so very brave, and a great warrior, but this giant is so big, he would squish you to mush before you even got a chance to take a good swing at him!'

'It's true!' said Fionn. 'But what am I to do? If I back out now I will seem like a coward.'

'Ah, you are no coward,' she smiled. 'Leave it to me, I have a plan. First you must build me a baby crib as big as a cow.'

'But our child has outgrown the crib. What need have we of a—'

'Trust me, husband, trust me,' she interrupted with a wink.

So Fionn did as she asked and built a wooden crib as big as a large milk cow.

'Now we will wait,' said Úna.

Meanwhile, over in Scotland, Benandonner was preparing for his fight. He put on his fighting kilt. He went to put on his favourite fighting boots but found one was missing (we know what happened, don't we?). This made him even angrier. He put on his second favourite pair of boots and began to build his half of the bridge to Ireland.

Úna and Fionn could hear his booming voice in the distance. They knew they had only half a day before he would be upon them.

Úna lit the stove and started baking a huge cake of soda bread. One half was normal, but into the other she put two horseshoes.

'I am coming for you, Fionn Mac Cumhaill,' roared Benandonner, 'and when I get to you I will squish you to mush!'

'Just like my cousin said!' squeaked Fionn.

Benandonner had reached the middle of the causeway, but there was no sign of Fionn.

'You can't escape me,' shouted the giant, 'I will come to your house and squish you to mush!' His voice was getting closer and closer.

'Quick! Put on this bonnet I made for you and get in the cradle!' said Úna.

Fionn jumped into the cradle, and no sooner was he in than the giant burst through the door.

'Where is he? Where is Fionn?' roared the giant.

'He's out,' said Úna, handing him a giant cup of tea made in a basin. 'Sure have a cuppa while you wait.'

Benandonner tossed the tea back into his mouth in a single sip.

Suddenly a terrible wail came from the back room of the cottage. It sounded like a whale or an elephant!

'Is that some kind of wild animal?' asked the giant.

'Not at all,' said Úna. 'It's just the baby.' And with that she lifted the huge cake of bread and a leg of mutton onto a wheelbarrow. 'I'm just going to tend to him. Come and see?'

'Surely you're not giving that big wheelbarrow of food to a baby for his lunch?' said the giant.

'Don't be silly,' laughed Úna. 'He's already eaten his lunch. This is just a little snack to keep him going until his dinner!' And she pushed open the door to the back room and wheeled in the wheelbarrow.

There, in the huge cradle, was Fionn, dressed as a baby. He grabbed the leg of mutton and began tearing into it with his teeth.

'N'YOM N'YOM N'YOM N'YOM!' said (Fionn) the baby! 'BURRRRRRRRRRRPPPPP!'

He let out a huge belch that was so strong it blew the giant's hair and beard up in the air.

'Oh, how rude of me,' said Úna, handing the giant half the soda cake. 'To go with your tea?'

Benandonner bit down on the cake and yelped – 'Ow!' – for little did he know that inside the cake was baked two horseshoes!

'Is it too chewy for you?' Úna asked. 'Baby likes it a bit chewy.' And she tossed the second half of the cake over to baby Fionn, who ate it no problem, as it had no horseshoes in it!

For the first time ever Benandonner the giant was afraid.

'What a big baby,' said the giant, laughing nervously.

'Ara not at all!' laughed Úna. 'Sure this little doteen is the runt of our litter – he's the smallest of the ten boys.'

'TEN boys?' gasped the giant.

'Yes indeed! And his ten sisters are even bigger!' smiled Úna.

With that the 'baby' picked up a huge basket of apples and tossed them at the giant, hitting him on the head with a thump. 'Ow!' Thump, thump. 'Ow!' THUMP!

'Play?' said the baby, in a deep gravelly voice.

'Emm. Nice baby … what a big baby!' said Benandonner, backing up towards the door. For in his head the giant was having many frightening thoughts.

It seemed like this Fionn Mac Cumhaill had a small army of children. A small army of HUGE children. What would they do if their father was defeated in battle? Surely they would want revenge. And if this apple-throwing, mutton-belching giant of a baby was the SMALLEST child of Fionn Mac Cumhaill, then what size must Fionn himself be?

Benandonner was deeply regretting his decision to challenge Fionn to a fight. He was deeply regretting building half a causeway to come over. He was deeply regretting sitting in that kitchen. He had to think fast!

'Emm, Mrs Mac Cumhaill?' said Benandonner. 'I'm afraid that tasting your beautiful soda bread has reminded me of something. I think I left my own bread baking on the griddle by mistake. I fear it may burn if I don't go back to Scotland right now!'

'Oh, you can't have that!' said Úna, smiling. 'There is nothing sadder than a good cake of bread spoiled. But are you sure you can't stay another few minutes? Fionn will be sorry he missed you.'

'No, no!' said Benandonner anxiously. 'Please give him my regards and regrets, but it would be a shame to burn my bread.'

'I understand,' said Úna. 'Say goodbye, baby.'

'Buuuuuuurrrrrrppppp!' Baby Fionn belched again with a belch so strong that it blew the front door open.

'Sure perhaps my husband can go visit ya later to sample your cake …' Una started to say – but Benandonner had seized the opportunity and run straight out the open door. Down the beach he ran, fast as he could! Boom, boom, boom went his giant footsteps, never stopping until he reached the great causeway. There, he took a single glance back, to see if the HUGE Fionn was following him.

Of course he wasn't, but Benandonner didn't know that.

As Benandonner began to make his way across the causeway, a terrible thought occurred to him.

'What if Úna's right? What if Fionn DOES decide to follow me across to Scotland? He'll do more than sample my soda cake – he will squish me to mush!'

And so Benandonner began to pull up huge pieces of the causeway behind him as he ran, tossing them deep into the sea.

'Now he can't follow me,' he said.

Of course, you and I know Fionn had no intention of following him. Fionn was delighted to be at home with his family, sitting by the fire, knowing that he would not be squished to mush that day.

'What a clever wife I have!' he said to Úna.

'And what a big baby I have,' she said, taking the bonnet off his head. 'No, wait,' she smiled, 'it's a perfectly sized husband!'

And they both laughed and laughed and laughed.

If you visit County Antrim in Ireland, you can still see the remains of the Giant's Causeway, with all the beautiful rocks that look like a beehive. And if you go down to the beach, you can still see the giant's boot too, where Fionn pushed it over the cliff. The old woman and her cat have long moved on though …

7

THE KING'S EARS

This is one of those stories that has many different versions. The one I would like to tell you here is a little less known and comes from County Cork. I heard it when I was small and visiting that part of the country on my holidays.

There is a lake called Lough Oighinn a few miles from the town of Skibbereen. In the middle of the lake there was once a castle, and in that castle lived a great king. He was of the O'Driscoll Clan and was a very powerful man.

This king had a secret, and he kept this secret all his life. The secret was his ears – they were not like usual human ears but rather long and hairy and floppy.

In fact, they looked just like the ears of a donkey!

The king had donkey's ears.

When he was a child, his mother hid his ears from the world with big hats, scarves, and sometimes even bonnets. He was hidden away from people and not allowed to go outside. He never had a chance to play with other children, and this made him angry. As he grew older his anger also grew, so much so that many in his court were afraid of him and his cruelty.

Now you might say to yourself, 'I like donkeys! They have nice cute ears.'

So why was it such a terrible thing to have donkey's ears? Why did the king's ears have to be hidden away from everyone?

Well, you see in those days, in order to be a king, you had to look very regular. If you had anything unusual like donkey's ears, or a tail, or a fish face, it meant that you couldn't be king. It was forbidden. They were a bit boring like that back then. It might be nice to have a king with a tail.

The king's mother did a good job of hiding this secret. He grew his hair long to keep his ears covered, and as he got older, nobody suspected a thing.

Now, having long hair was fine and not that unusual, but every now and then he had to have a haircut, just to take a little bit off it, and keep it healthy. The only person allowed to cut the king's hair was his mother, of course, as she already knew his secret.

As years passed though, his mother grew very old and her hands grew stiff. The day came when they were too stiff to use a pair of scissors, but the king still needed his haircut.

The king summoned a young barber from a neighbouring town. It was a great honour to be asked to the castle, and the barber was delighted with himself. He sharpened his best scissors, put them in his pouch, and set off on the walk down past Lough Oighinn, towards the castle. When he arrived, he was met by a very serious-looking king.

'You are here to cut my hair, and that is all,' said the king. 'Anything you see here will be our secret. Do you understand?'

Of course, the barber had no idea what the king was on about. Perhaps he had greasy hair or dandruff? What was this big secret that the king had, he wondered?

'Of course, your majesty,' said the barber. 'Sure I've seen all sorts of hair; long, short, greasy, flaky, fluffy, patchy, scratchy, and thin. Any secret is safe with me.'

The barber pulled out his pouch of scissors and sat the king down on a chair with a towel around his shoulders. He could tell the king was nervous.

He lifted up a big lock of the king's hair between his fingers. 'No need to worry, your majesty; sure your hair is lovely and healthy, and it—'

He stopped speaking very suddenly. There, underneath the lock of hair, was of course a donkey's ear!

'Tee hee hee … emm … cough, cough, cough.' He couldn't help it, when he saw the donkey's ear, the barber let out a little giggle, but quickly changed it to make it sound like he was coughing.

'Apologies, your majesty,' the barber added. 'I'm just getting over a bad cold.'

But the king wasn't fooled.

The barber finished cutting the king's hair and fixed it so it once again covered the donkey's ears. He packed up his pouch of scissors and razors, and the king paid him his coin, but said nothing.

As the barber walked back towards his home, he let the smile appear on his face again, and this time let out a bigger giggle as there was nobody around. 'The king has donkey's ears,' he thought, then he giggled out loud. 'Tee hee hee …'

No sooner did he let the giggle out of his mouth, than out of the bushes appeared two of the king's soldiers. Without a word they picked up the barber and tossed him in the lake.

And that was the end of him.

You see, the king did not trust a man who laughed at his ears to keep his secret. If he found it that funny, surely he would tell another? He'd instructed his soldiers to grab the barber on his way home and throw him in the lake.

'He gave me a terrible haircut,' he told them, in case they questioned his reason.

But, of course, they wouldn't – they were afraid of their king.

On the spot where the soldiers threw the barber in the lake, a patch of reeds began to grow.

The king has donkey's ears.

The people in the town all wondered what had happened to the barber for a while. Then they stopped wondering. Some said he had travelled to a bigger town or a city where people paid more for their haircuts.

'He's gone for a better life,' they said.

But, of course, that wasn't true.

The king has donkey's ears.

Years later, the king decided to hold a great party at the castle. He invited other kings, noble people and guests from all over the country. He wanted to show off what a great king he was. He wanted to show everyone what likeable he was (which, of course, he wasn't).

All the best musicians from the county were commanded to play, so they got busy practicing their tunes, polishing their instruments, and getting ready for the party.

The king's Uilleann piper selected his very best set of pipes to play. Uilleann pipes are a beautiful instrument, and all the little parts of the instrument need to be looked after well.

The piper carefully polished the chanter, adjusted the drones, and checked that everything was working perfectly. He decided he needed to replace the reeds in the pipe (where the sound is made), so off he went down to Lough Oighinn to cut himself some reeds to fit the pipes.

Down at the lakeside he spotted some lovely strong reeds and collected a few for his pipes. It was the very spot where the barber had been tossed in the lake, but of course nobody but the king and the soldiers knew that.

The night of the party, all of the important guests arrived at the castle. There was plenty of food and drink for everyone, and the king overheard someone say how generous he was. Perhaps now he would be liked by more people, and not just feared.

The music started and everyone was having a great time. The king's piper sat in on the music session and took out his best pipes – the ones with the new reeds from the lake.

He pumped the bellows full of air and began to play. No sooner had he started, than the strangest thing happened. Instead of music coming from the pipes, a voice was heard. A sad, singing voice.

The fiddler stopped fiddling, the flautist stopped fluting, and all the people stopped dancing. But the piper kept playing, as that

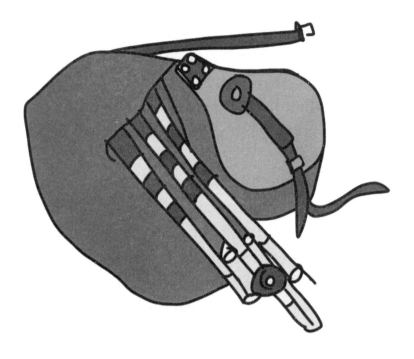

is what his pipes wanted. And from deep within the pipes a voice sang:

The king has donkey's ears!
The king has donkey's ears!
The king has donkey's ears!

Many people recognised it as the voice of the barber. Everyone was silent. They all stared at the king.

The king began to shake his head as if to deny it, but the more he shook his head, the more his hair tossed about, until, finally, his carefully hidden ears popped out!

The king has donkey's ears!
The king has donkey's ears!
The king has donkey's ears!

The people began to sing along, as they laughed and pointed at the king.

The king has donkey's ears!
The king has donkey's ears!
The king has donkey's ears!

He had lost the respect of his people and could no longer be king.

He may have tried to hide his secret deep in the waters of the lake, but the lake decided it was time to reveal his true nature.

And what the lake wants, the lake gets …

The king has donkey's ears!
The king has donkey's ears!
The king has donkey's ears!

8

CAKE

In the county of Galway there are loads of lovely places to go for a walk. I live in Galway City and if we have visitors coming, we always recommend people go for a walk on 'the Prom'; the Salthill Promenade.

All year round you will see people walking their dogs – and sometimes their cats! You'll see people swimming up at Blackrock Tower, meeting friends for coffee, and, of course, people watching. Sunday is a particularly good day to people watch. Folks usually start the walk in town, go all the way to Blackrock and 'kick the wall'. Then turn around and go back. Now they are not angry at the wall or anything, it is just a tradition that many people follow to mark the middle point of their walk.

Another thing you'll notice when walking the Prom is the seagulls. We have a lot of them. Some are very cheeky too, and if you're not careful, they will swoop down and steal one of your chips or a bit of your chocolate, or sometimes (if they're big enough), they'll steal a whole sandwich, right out of your hand! They are very squawky, these sandwich thieves, and it really sounds like they are trying to tell you something.

And do you know what? Some of them are!

About a hundred years ago, in Galway, there lived two sisters; Áine and Máire Casey. Like most sisters, some days they liked each other, and other days they had big squabbles. Mostly though, they got along like a house on fire and were great friends. They liked many of the same interests and

liked to do these things together when they could. One of their favourite things to do was to take a picnic to Salthill Prom on a Sunday to people watch.

This particular Sunday was no different. The sisters set out, armed with their usual picnic supplies: a wicker basket, a cloth tablecloth, cheese sandwiches wrapped in paper, and a bottle of hot sweet tea. Before we had thermos flasks, many people used to carry hot tea in a glass bottle. Did you know that?

In that basket, the sisters had one extra thing – a dessert from their Auntie Nora; a big slice of her special fruitcake for the sisters to share. Now it wasn't often they got it. At that time, it was said that there was no better fruitcake in the whole county than the one made by Nora, so this really was a special treat. Máire and Áine were really looking forward to it.

Down at the Prom, the sun was out, but there was a wind, and the waves were choppy. The sisters set out their blanket by the water. The sea air made them hungry, and it wasn't long before they had devoured their sandwiches and washed them down with tea.

They sat back and watched all the people go by – children playing with their ball, an old man walking his dog, a couple holding hands, and, of course, the handsome lads who would maybe tip their caps at the girls and nod!

They were enjoying a sup of tea, when who should appear in the distance but Seán Walsh. Now Máire really liked Seán, and Seán liked Máire, and whenever they got the chance, they would flirt with each other by trying to make the other one laugh. It was a bit of a competition between them in fact, to see who could make the other laugh the loudest! They'd be in the market place and Máire would turn to Seán and puff out her cheeks like a balloon. Or even in the church on Sunday, Seán would turn to Máire sitting in the pew behind, pull at the end of his nose and make a pig snout!

Father O'Brien wasn't too happy and would frown at their giggles.

Well anyway, when Máire saw Seán walking up the Prom, she saw her chance to make him laugh. In a split second didn't she grab the WHOLE piece of Auntie Nora's fruitcake and shove it in her mouth. Just as Seán passed, she opened her mouth with all the cake inside and made a face. Ooooh it was pretty disgusting, with bits of cake and raisins falling out the side of her mouth! It looked like a big pit of slurry. Of course, Seán thought this was hilarious and started roaring laughing!

Will I'll tell you who WASN'T laughing? Áine, that's who!

She had been looking forward ALL day to that fruitcake from Auntie Nora. Half of it was for her after all! But her so-and-so of a sister had gone and shoved the WHOLE thing in her mouth, just to show off to STUPID Seán Walsh.

Áine had a hot temper, and this was a day to test it. She was so annoyed at her sister that, without thinking, didn't she stand up and SLAP Máire across the face! Ouch!

Well, all the bits of cake went flying out of Máire's mouth in slow motion, and the force of the slap spun her head to the side.

Seán Walsh took off like a light. There was no way he was sticking around for what was coming next. He ran off up the Prom, and over his head storm clouds began to gather and rain began to fall.

I told you that Áine had a hot temper; well, will I tell you who had one twice as bad? Maybe you can guess? Máire, that's who. She could feel the blood rushing to her stinging cheek where her sister had slapped her. But she could also feel this temper rising up through her body, like a dark red wave. She was furious, and do you know what? She was SO furious that again, without thinking, she lifted her arms and pushed her sister into the deep sea!

Oh no!

Of course, Máire immediately regretted what she had done. She reached out to help her sister, but the waves were too rough now. The weather had changed and become stormy, and Máire was not a strong swimmer. She turned to get help, but Séan was long gone, and the whole Promenade was now deserted of people as the rain poured down.

'Help!' cried Máire. 'Somebody please help me save my sister!'

But there was nobody around, and Máire watched her sister go under the waves for the first time. Máire felt so desperate that she began to wail!

'It's all my fault. Me and my stupid jokes and fooling with Seán Walsh. If it hadn't been for me shoving that cake in me mouth, my sister wouldn't be in the sea!'

Máire began to pray and wish with everything in her body. She wished so hard that her words became a sort of spell, and the bigger and bigger her promises, the stronger this spell got.

'I'll do anything!' she said. 'If anyone or anything can hear me? If you save my sister's life, I will never joke around with Seán Walsh again. I will never joke around with anyone! I will never marry, and I promise to walk this Prom until the end of my days repenting. Please, just save my dear sister!'

Well, somehow, someone or something heard her wish …

Out in the water, as Áine sunk down beneath the waves for a second time, the strangest things began to happen to her. Out from the tips of her fingers, tiny white feathers began to sprout.

Ping, ping, ping, ping, ping. Ping, ping, ping, ping, ping!

Then the same down along her arms and her back.

Ping, ping, ping, ping, ping. Ping, ping, ping, ping, ping!

Her legs grew narrow and the toes of her feet began to web together.

Her mouth changed shape – her lips grew hard and yellow and pointy.

And just as she dipped beneath the waves for the third time, she turned and

rose up out of the water, and into the air –
as a seagull!

Máire let out a cry of relief. Seagull or no
seagull, her sister hadn't drowned, she was
alive. She was so happy!

I'll tell you who wasn't happy though!
Áine! A seagull? *A seagull?* She didn't want
to be a seagull! She flew over to her sister
and began to peck at her in anger, but Máire
just stood and smiled.

Well, Máire did indeed keep her promise. From that day forth, she never showed off or joked with Seán Walsh (or to any other lad for that matter), she never married, and she spent the rest of her days walking up and down the Salthill Promenade. You would see her, even as an old woman, walking there, a bird circling her head. Sometimes pecking, sometimes swooping down to feed on the sandwiches she fed it from her pocket.

When she passed away and was laid out in her coffin, there, sat on top of it, was a seagull – pecking, pecking, pecking away.

Now it's been many years since the day of that picnic, and Máire is long gone. But to this day if you are walking in Salthill, and you look up, you might see Áine still. She'll be flying up above you, as a seagull, swooping and squawking. And if you listen carefully, you'll hear her tell you, over and over, about the one thing that started it all:

'Caaaakkkke!'

'Caaakke!'

'Cake!'

9

THE WATERS OF IRELAND

'Tis a pleasure to meet you? Have we met before?
I've possibly knocked on your grand-mother's door.

If you heard singing, when you played as a child,
Near the rushes or blackthorn, or flowers that grow wild.

Or if you heard thunderous sounds from a cave,

Well, that was me saying hello with a wave.

I usually favour environments cool,
But I warmed up in Mallow, exception
to rule!

I'm black and I'm white and I'm brown
on my head,
Occasionally too, I may even be red.

I've carried brave queens and parlayed
with some kings,
I've seen many lifetimes of wonderful
things.

I've wandered through villages, cities
and towns,
From Cape Clear to Galway, from
Wicklow to Down.

There are so many places that I can call
home,
And though often I settle, more often I
roam.

In Owey I live both above and below,
In the Burren I'm busy so I may just go.

I've been noted as beautiful, ugly and deep,
I've been known to steal maidens away
as they sleep.

I'm powerful, I'm nimble, I'm angry, I'm
still,
I can leap from a mountain and race
down a hill.

I've jumped from a height in the Glen
of Kilfane,
And in Assaranca, I still do the same.

Some may have guessed who I am by
and by,
I am one, I am many and that is no lie.

For those who can't see it, sure harbour
no shame,
For the Waters of Ireland have many a
name.

10

THE FAIRY SHIP OF ROSES

Ah, this is one of my favourite stories. In fact, it is a story within a song within a story (I'll even put a note about the song in the back of this book for you, in case you want to learn it later). The song can be sung all in one go, but for this book I am going to sprinkle the verses throughout it, so they happen in time with the story. You can leave them out, put them in, change the tune, whatever you like!

Once upon a time, in a city in the west of Ireland, there lived a young man. His family had moved there from a distant town and didn't have much money to their name.

Now the young man had fallen head over heels in love with a certain young maiden in the town, and she had fallen in love with him too. She was the daughter of a rich merchant, and her family had a lot of money. When the young man went to the merchant and asked if he could marry his daughter, the merchant laughed.

'Who do you think you are, young man? You are too poor! Of course you can't marry my daughter; how would you provide for her and buy her fine clothes and jewels?'

The maiden herself tried to persuade her father that she didn't need all these fine things, that she would be happy enough with just the young man and nothing else. But her father was hearing none of it.

So, the young man headed off into the town, trying to find odd jobs, so he could prove his worth to the merchant, and perhaps marry the maiden. Deep down he knew though, that even with these odd jobs, he would make so little money that he would be an old man before he had enough wealth to marry his beloved.

That night, as he walked along the shore, kicking the stones with his feet, he could feel his heart, heavy and aching, pining for his love. As he walked along the water's edge, something unusual caught his attention. He noticed a strange fog out on the horizon – he had never seen anything like it. He also noticed that there were fewer people about than usual. The few he did see seemed to be couples in love holding hands very tightly, and this made him feel even sadder.

What he didn't realise was that the fog out at sea had a special name. It was known as 'the Pining Fog' and it was a dangerous thing indeed! Now some older locals knew of the legend of the Pining Fog (and were afraid of it, so remained indoors). Others, like the young man, were from other towns, or were simply too young to have heard the legend.

Oh, perhaps I should tell you about the legend too?

Well, the story goes that a thousand years in the past there lived a fairy prince and princess. They were very much in love, but because they came from two different fairy clans (who were at war with each other), they were forbidden to marry. The prince and princess devised a secret plan to run away together, but a servant overheard them talking and went and told the fairy king.

The night of the elopement, the king cast a spell. He summoned a huge ship out on the sea, made entirely from magical roses. He put the princess on the ship and bound the ship with an enchantment. This made sure that the ship would never be able to dock on any land in any place. Around the ship was wrapped a thick fog, so that no light would ever pass through, and the ship would remain hidden from all (including the prince).

Every ship needs a crew though, so once every hundred years, the Pining Fog itself would roll in to the shore for one day. It would seek out any mortal man with an aching heart, enchant him, and take him back to work for the rest of his days on the Fairy Ship of Roses.

And that is how legend of the Pining Day got its name, for when the fog landed, it only chose those with sadness in their hearts – those who were pining for love – to take back to work on the ship.

Now many people said, 'sure the Pining Day is just an old legend!' But there were other people, particularly older people, who still believed in it. They spoke about a very old man, the oldest man you could imagine, who walked into a tavern one day, and just before he died, he asked for one last drink. He claimed to have been taken by the Pining Fog and had worked on the Fairy Ship of Roses for a hundred years. He was very thirsty!

Then there were the sailors who claimed when far out at sea in a deep fog, that they had passed by the fairy ship, and although they could never see it, they could smell the overpowering scent of thousands of roses as the ship sailed past.

But what of our young man back in our story, standing on the dock? Well, I'll tell you this: at that moment, as he stood on the shore with his aching heart, the enchanted fog did indeed roll in. It lifted the young man off the dock and carried him far out to sea to the Fairy Ship of Roses! So yes, the legend of the Pining Day was true, and it had just claimed another poor crew member …

> While walking on the Pining Day,
> A young man he got stole away,
> Stole away forever to the Fairy Ship of Roses.
>
> Where is my love, please tell to me?
> He's gone off sailing on the sea.
> He's gone off sailing on the sea,
> On the Fairy Ship of Roses.
>
> Fog took him from the Shaley shore,
> Now he will see his love no more.
> He'll spend his days a-rigging sails,
> On the Fairy Ship of Roses.

Well, some fishermen on their boats spotted the fog arrive and take the young man away. The word spread, and by afternoon, the news reached the maiden that her beloved was gone! Her father tried to console her, but she just wept and wept. In fact, she wept until her woolen shawl became so heavy with tears that it brought her to her knees.

But she didn't give up hope.

That night, while her parents were sleeping, she climbed out her window, went down to the dock, stole a small boat and began to row out into the wild sea! She didn't know where she was going. All she knew is that she had to find her true love …

The news it reached the maiden's ears,
And she could not contain her tears,
She took a boat and off she rowed, to the Fairy Ship of Roses.

Where is my love, please tell to me?
He's gone off sailing on the sea.
He's gone off sailing on the sea,
On the Fairy Ship of Roses.

The boat was tossed around the waves,
But still the maiden, she was brave.
The fog so thick, 'twould make you sick,
At the Fairy Ship of Roses.

Brave though the maiden was, the waves grew taller and taller around the little boat. They tossed her to and fro, threatening to capsize her. The fog was so thick that she couldn't see her own hand in front of her when she held it up.

'This is it!' she thought. 'I am ready to meet my end'. She closed her eyes, and tried to soothe herself with her own thoughts. She imagined herself and the young man embracing. She could feel her heart filling with so much love that she felt she might explode.

Then the strangest thing happened. From deep within her heart a light began to shine. It grew brighter and brighter, until it surrounded her like a huge red flame. This light was so powerful, so strong, that it began to burn through the enchanted fog and melt it away. As the fog wafted up into the night sky, she saw it! There it was, right in front of her – the Fairy Ship of Roses!

It was at once both terrifying and beautiful. It rose up from the sea, as tall as the tallest building. There were hundreds and thousands of red roses woven together to make up its hull, mast, and sail, with a single white rose for a flag.

The maiden tethered her boat to a rose vine and began to climb up one side of the ship. She was just a few feet up when a huge wave came, snapped the vine, and tossed her boat away into the dark seas. Now there was no going back, no escaping. Her only hope was to keep on climbing.

It seemed an impossible task. The roses came away in her hands as she climbed, and many times she almost fell back into the raging sea! There were sharp thorns that dug deep into her skin and tore at her clothes, but that didn't stop her, she kept on climbing! Finally, when she was almost too tired to reach the top, she lifted herself up one last time, and with a great heave of strength, landed on the deck of the ship!

Right in front of her was the fairy princess, standing at the bow, and looking out to sea with great sadness in her eyes. The maiden turned around, and there, beside her, stood her beloved young man. When he saw her, it was as if he had just woken from a deep sleep, and he rushed to embrace her.

'My fair maiden,' he said, 'you have found me.'

'It was my heart,' she said, 'it was my heart that found you …'

> The maiden's heart burned fiery bright,
> Like a beacon in the blackest night,
> The fog it vanished out of sight,
> By the Fairy Ship of Roses.
>
> Where is my love, please tell to me?
> He's gone off sailing on the sea.
> He's gone off sailing on the sea,
> On the Fairy Ship of Roses.
>
> She climbed up petal and up thorn.
> Her petticoat and her shawl were torn.
> She saw her true love's face that morn,
> On the Fairy Ship of Roses.

The two were so overjoyed to be with each other! But now they were both trapped on the ship, as the enchantment would never let it reach land, remember? And what of the poor fairy princess, she was still heartbroken. She had been trapped on the ship for over a thousand years without her prince! This was such a sad state of affairs.

But you'll never guess what happened next!

Suddenly, from across the waves, the sound of galloping horses' hooves could be heard. 'Thikka thump, thikka thump, thikka thump, thikka thump, thikka thump ...'

The princess's eyes lit up – for there, galloping across the waves on a huge white horse, was her beloved fairy prince!

You see, because the fog had been lifted, the prince was able to see the ship again after all these years. He had never stopped looking for his princess. When he reached the ship, he leapt off his horse, onto the deck, and embraced his true love the princess – for the first time in a thousand years!

The prince thanked the maiden from the bottom of his heart for lifting the fog and reuniting him with his true love. He asked if he could do anything to repay her. She told him the story of how she and her beloved

could never wed because the lad was poor and had no prospects.

The fairy prince smiled. He took off his royal chain from around his neck, and placed it around the young man's neck instead. This chain was very beautiful. It was made from the brightest gold you had ever seen, decorated with jewels as bright as the stars in the sky; diamonds, rubies, emeralds and more!

'Take this,' the prince said, 'it is the least I can do to thank you both. It is also enchanted with the spell of plenty. Each time you pluck a jewel from the gold, a new one will grow back in its place. You are rich now, and will never want for money again.'

The young couple were very thankful. Now that the young man was wealthy, he could marry his beloved back in their village.

'Alas, how will we return to shore?' the young man said. 'The ship is enchanted so it will never again touch land.'

'Ah,' said the prince. 'I have a solution. I will give to you my faithful horse, so you and your maiden may reach the shore. She is powerful and magical; and can gallop over fire, over air, over land and over sea – but she is long overdue a rest! She carried me to the four corners of the earth for a thousand years, as I searched the seas for my true love.'

The fairy princess smiled and shed a tear of happiness.

'Thank you,' said the young man. 'I will take good care of your horse and give her plenty of rest back on the land.'

The young man and the maiden waved goodbye to the prince and princess. They climbed up on the back of the beautiful fairy horse, and set off for the shore.

As they galloped across the waves, the maiden whispered sadly to her young man, 'But what about them, my love, what about them?'

A fairy steed came racing o'er,
And took the lovers back to shore,
They'd not return for evermore, to the
Fairy Ship of Roses.

Where is my love, please tell to me?
He's gone off sailing on the sea.
He's gone off sailing on the sea,
On the Fairy Ship of Roses.

And now my love, that I found thee,
No more a sailing on the sea,
You'll spend your nights at home with
me,
Not the Fairy Ship of Roses.

And that's almost the end of the song.
　But what of the maiden's question?
　What of the fairy prince and princess?
　Without a horse, they had no way to
reach the shore themselves?
　What was to be their fate?
　Well, as time moves differently for fairy
folk, even though it had been a thousand
years in our world, in the fairy realm their
two fairy families were, alas, still at war with
each other. The fairy prince and princess
decided that they would stay onboard the
ship for another thousand years.

Perhaps, then, there would be peace between their families. Perhaps the beautiful horse, once rested, would return for her prince and the princess. Perhaps it would take more than a thousand years. But you know what, they didn't mind, because now, at last, they were together …

Where are we love, please tell to me?
We're still a sailing on the sea,
Forever on the waves we'll be
On the Fairy Ship of Roses.

11

WARTS AND ALL

There are loads of places in Ireland that are supposed to have 'watery cures' for things. Places where you dip in the water or sometimes drink it to make you feel better. These are often in the form of 'holy wells', 'sacred wells' or 'magic wells'.

I was very happy to find out though, that these magical waters can even include a puddle! Yes, a puddle!

There is an area in County Clare, in the west of Ireland, called the Burren. I mention it in a few stories myself. It is quite a special place for a number of reasons (and some wonderful stories come from there). In the Burren, much of the rock is made from limestone. There are many beautiful flowers that grow in the cracks of this limestone, and in fact, some of these flowers don't grow anywhere else in the world! It's a mighty place for a walk, and I hope you get to visit it sometime if you haven't already.

If you went for a walk there on a Tuesday evening, and if you passed a certain hill, you might see someone sticking their thumb in a puddle!

Hmmm.

Or if you went there on a Wednesday night, to the same hill, you might spy someone with their socks off and their feet stuck in.

Hmmm.

What's going on, you might wonder? So did I. Until I discovered the answer! Apparently, these people are up on the side of this particular hill for what's known as 'the Warty Cure'.

For on this particular hill there is a tiny pool of water. To tell you the truth, it is not even big enough to be a pond, so the best name for it would be a puddle. Some say it is fed by an underground spring, some say it is just the rain gathered in a dip in the rock.

Puddle

It is said (and has been said for many years) that if you find this particular puddle, and if you have a wart you want to get rid of, you can do so by dunking the wart in this puddle!

Now when I heard of this, I had a lot of questions: If the wart is on your nose, do you stick your whole head in the puddle? Do you have to hold your breath? If the wart is on the top of your head, do you have to do a headstand? Do people even get warts on the top of their heads? What if the wart is on your bottom? Do you have to sit in the puddle? Is the puddle big enough for people with large bottoms?

So many questions!

One thing is for sure, people still go walking in the Burren, and they still go looking for 'the Warty Cure' puddle. If you go there, perhaps you can find out the answers to all my questions, and perhaps you can bring back some stories too!

12

THE KING AND THE MERMAID

There are many old stories that tell of a magical island that is to be found off the west coast of Ireland. Some say this island is enchanted, and can only appear to human eyes every seven years.

Some call this island 'Brasil' ('Brasil' that rhymes with 'dazzle' not 'Brasil' that rhymes with 'hill' – the second one might be a country in South America that you can get to just fine any day of the week if you live nearby, or you can take an aeroplane!).

This island was also called 'Hy-Brasil', and in fact, if you look at very old maps of Ireland, drawn hundreds of years ago, there does appear to be an extra island there! Some people say the island disappeared forever when a fiery volcano erupted and it sank deep beneath the wild waves. Other people say the island is still there, it is just not for everyone to see.

Once there was a lion, a powerful lion like no other you have ever seen. He was the King of the Fire Realm; a kingdom in the middle of the sea, built around a towering volcano. He walked his walks with a tall and majestic air. His lion's roar was loud and beautiful, like the rumble of a volcano dipped in honey. His eyes glowed like hot coals, and his mane was made of pure flame; flickering bursts of amber, orange, and yellow. He was the most beautiful creature anyone had ever seen – and well he knew it!

Each day the lion would walk to the ocean. He would walk along the shores of his kingdom, admiring his own reflection in the seawater. And it was indeed a beautiful sight. Even the fish would stop swimming to gaze up at the flickering reflection of his mane.

One day, the lion was walking along the shore when he stopped suddenly in his tracks. There, out in the ocean, was the most beautiful creature that he had ever seen. She was a mermaid, with eyes the colour of the twinkling stars, skin like fresh cream, and hair the colour of the softest moss.

The lion was speechless.

The mermaid looked to the shore and saw the lion looking at her. She felt her heart heat up with the warmth of love. He too was the most beautiful creature that she had ever seen, and she wanted nothing more in that moment than to embrace him.

The mermaid stretched out her hand and beckoned the lion to swim to her. The lion felt his heart fill with the warmth of love, and began to walk into the ocean. But just as he was about to leave his depth and swim to her, he happened to glance down and catch his own reflection in the water. He saw the likeness of his beautiful mane of fire dancing back at him, and he knew that if he took another step, the seawater would quench his mane.

He knew that if he took another step, his mane of flame would become like that of any other lion.

He knew that if he took another step, he would become ordinary – no longer the most beautiful creature of all.

He stopped.

He looked at the mermaid, and their eyes met. There was such love between them. But instead of swimming to her, the lion turned away and began to walk back to the shores of his kingdom. His vanity had ruled his heart, and though he had felt great love, he could not bring himself to quench his fiery mane.

As he walked away, there was a great cracking sound. It was the sound of the mermaid's heart breaking in two. It was a sound so sharp, so strong, that it shook the water around her and caused a great tidal wave to rise up from the depths. The wave was both powerful and fast, and in the blink of an eye it was upon the lion, and had not only quenched his mane, but had torn it right off his head, and swept it far out to sea!

The lion turned just in time to see the mermaid slip in between the waves, her tears of sadness washing into the water as she swam away. The lion knew then that he had made the wrong decision, but it was too late, the mermaid was gone. He was left standing there alone, with no mane at all.

As he plodded back to the shore, bald and dejected, he made a vow that he would search every day for the mermaid. Perhaps one day he would find her, and if he did, he would beg her forgiveness for his wrong decision. Perhaps she would forgive him, and they could be together, as of course they were always meant to be.

The lion's mane was washed far out into the ocean. As it tossed about in the waves, it began to multiply, and change into a thousand tiny creatures. These creatures drifted around the oceans, and washed up on the shores of many lands, particularly those where the water was cooler, like our shores in Ireland.

Now to this very day, if you walk on our beaches, you may well come across one of these creatures. If you do, you must be very careful, for trapped within each one is the sting of the mermaid's heartbreak. A sorrow so powerful that even after thousands of years it still holds its sting, and if you were to touch it or step on it, you too would experience that sting.

The local people in many lands know this mane, and know that each part is a living thing. They have given it the name 'the Lion's Mane Jellyfish'.

But what of the king – the great lion that once walked with a mane of flame?

Well, try as he might, he could never find his beloved mermaid. The ocean is vast though, and to this day he continues to search for her. In order to swim the great distances in his search, he must eat huge numbers of fish to give him strength, and his body has grown round and oily to keep him warm in the cold waters.

He is grumpy, for he has not yet found the mermaid, and you will often hear him roar. But his roar is no longer dipped in honey. It has become rough from the salty seawater. His head no longer holds his mane of flame. He is still as bald as the day the great wave of sadness quenched it and plucked it from his head. He is still a lion, but now he is a lion of the sea. In France they call him the *lion de mer*.

In Ireland we call him the *leon farraige*.
The lion of the sea.
The sea lion.

13

BLACK AND WHITE

Every weekend, ever since she was a very little girl, Tara would ask her father the same question:

'Daddy, will I see a fairy in the garden today?'

Her father would just chuckle and shrug his shoulders. He was a nice man, but he was very practical, and he didn't believe in 'silly things' like fairies (his words). Tara knew this because she overheard her dad say it to her mam one night when they were talking in the kitchen.

If he was tired or stressed out, he wouldn't shrug but would frown or make a grumbly sound at the back of his throat. Shrugging your shoulders or grumbling wasn't a 'no', and that was good enough for her. There was still a chance!

Tara loved Saturday breakfast with her dad. He was a busy man during the week. He worked in a big office in the middle of Cork City, and had a very important job. On weekdays, he was always in a rush, and sometimes only had time to grab a slice of toast for breakfast as he ran out the door.

But Saturdays were different. On Saturdays he could relax, sit back, have a big breakfast with orange juice, THREE cups of tea, and enjoy the newspaper while Tara sat beside him. He loved doing the crossword, and would sometimes ask Tara to help him with the clues. She knew her answers weren't the right ones, but she liked helping anyway. She watched as her father wrote the letters carefully into the black and white puzzle.

When she was a bit older, things started to change. Her dad's job seemed to get harder, and he had to work longer hours. Her Mam said it meant that they could afford a bigger car, but none of them really seemed to want a bigger car, so Tara was confused.

The worst thing was the weekends. Her dad often had to go into his office in the city to work on a Saturday. Tara missed their long breakfasts together, and she never did the crosswords by herself.

Sometimes though, Tara's Mam would take Tara to Cork to do some shopping on a Saturday. They would stop into her dad's office and take him coffee and something to eat. He was very busy, but he would try to take a break and sit with them.

Tara would ask the question she always asked.

'Daddy, will I see a fairy in the garden today?'

Her dad would still smile and shrug while eating his sandwich, but his smile wasn't as big any more.

This one particular Saturday when they popped in to see him, Tara knew something wasn't right. Her dad had a big frown and his papers were all over his desk. When they arrived, he told his wife he didn't have time for a break, but she insisted.

'Fifteen minutes, Eoin. You have to eat.'

She put tea and a sandwich on his desk and he took a big hungry bite of the sandwich.

Tara thought chatting might take his mind off work, so she asked him her usual question about fairies. But today was different. Instead of shrugging, he answered her.

'Tara, you're getting to be too old for this game now, so you are. Sometimes things are more black and white than you think in this world!'

She was very surprised at his answer. What did he mean 'black and white'? Black and white like a crossword puzzle?

'But Daddy, isn't there a chance I might see a fairy?' she asked.

As she said this, she threw her hands out with excitement, to make her point, and in doing so, didn't she knock her dad's cup of tea all over the papers on his desk! Her parents scrambled to mop up the spill with napkins.

'Sorry, Daddy,' said Tara, 'I didn't mean—'

But it was too late, her dad was very angry. 'Fairies?' he said. 'A chance?' His voice was shaking. 'Look,' he said, 'there's as much chance of you seeing fairies in our garden as …'

He looked around his office, as if to find something practical to use as an example. He glanced out the window at the River Lee flowing past outside, and he had what he needed …

'There's about as much chance of you seeing fairies, Tara, as there is me seeing a killer whale swimming up the river!'

He was out of breath. He felt sorry he had gotten so annoyed, but it was too late. He saw the look on Tara's face. It was as if someone had switched off a very bright light and switched on a duller one.

'Look, sweetheart …' he said, trying to fix it.

'It's all right, Daddy,' said Tara. 'I understand now.'

For her dad hadn't actually said no to her question, but he might as well have.

Her mam threw a frown at her husband over her shoulder. He shrugged and mouthed an 'I'm sorry' as he watched them walk out the door.

A few years went by.

Tara's dad got a different job in the same building, so he was less stressed out going to work. He still worked on Saturdays though.

Tara still looked out the window of her bedroom onto the hillside in the morning, but it was different now. All she saw was the scenery, and beautiful and all as it was, her gaze didn't linger as long. She'd even stopped visiting her dad for lunch in town, even though he had a bit more time now. She was older and had her friends to hang out with. She didn't think about it too much because when she did it made her a bit sad. She wasn't sure why.

It was the summer before she was due to start secondary school. This was an exciting time, as she would make lots of new friends and have new teachers. Because it was the last year of 'juniors', Tara and her friends were determined to make the most out of the summer, and went into town a lot more, particularly at weekends, where they would walk around, listening to the street music and looking at the shops.

It was the middle of June (Saturday the 16th to be precise!) and everyone was in a great mood. Tara's Mam went off shopping and told her she would meet her back at the car. Tara and her friends walked around the city, strolling with their ice pops. It seemed particularly busy that Saturday. They noticed there was a huge crowd of people over by the bank of the river. They were making a lot of noise, talking and pointing.

Tara was too short to see over the heads of the crowd, so she asked a lady what was going on.

'It's a whale!' said the woman excitedly.

'Two killer whales!' a man beside her chimed in.

'No! Three of them!' shouted a young boy from the front.

Killer whales?

Tara's heart was racing. She was normally very polite with queues and that sort of thing, but she couldn't help herself. She pushed in between the gaps in the crowd and up to the wall of the riverbank.

It was true! There they were, in the middle of the River Lee, on a Saturday afternoon in June – three Orca whales. Black and white and beautiful. People were so excited!

But Tara's mind was somewhere else. She thought about her dad. She thought about that day when he got angry in his office; she thought about what he said about impossible things, like a whale in the river! She thought about how much she missed spending time with him.

She took one more glance at the beautiful whales in the river and backed out through the crowd. She ran into the nearest shop and bought two sandwiches with her pocket money, and then walked down to where her dad worked. He could see the river from his window and she was sure he would be very surprised by the whales. They could eat lunch together and talk about it.

Just as she walked up to the door of his office though, who should she meet but her dad! He was rushing out the door and he had a bag in his hand with what looked like sandwiches.

'Tara!' he said.

'Dad!' she said. 'Emm … I was bringing you lunch. I wanted to show you something.'

'I can't have lunch,' said her Dad, 'I am too busy!'

Tara's face fell. 'Oh.'

But it was only for a moment.

'I'm too busy,' he said, 'because I've taken the rest of the day off to spend with my daughter. I've just seen three whales swim up the River Lee, so we'd better hurry!'

Tara beamed a big smile. 'Why are we in a hurry, Dad?'

'So we can get a good seat in the garden to eat our sandwiches!' he said. 'We don't want to waste any more time. Now that the whales have arrived, we don't want to miss catching a glimpse of those fairies!'

14

SEVEN TIMES ROUND

Do you know the way some people are related to each other? The way some people might have aunts and uncles and cousins living in different parts of the country, or indeed in different parts of the world than them?

Well, it's a bit like that with some stories. Even though they may be found far apart, they are somehow connected. A person or a place mentioned in one story might pop up in another story. An adventure told in one tale might be very similar to an adventure from another, even if they happened thousands of miles apart.

It's funny that way.

When you are reading or listening to stories, try to see if you recognise any of the characters or places. Do they belong to a bigger story family or are they like a snowflake and one of a kind?

Many place names in Ireland have a story behind them. If you visit a place, ask someone about the name. Is there a story behind it? And do you know what, even if there isn't, you can make up your own!

Do you know the story of Fionn and the Salmon of Knowledge (hint: you can read it in this book)? Well, this little story is a cousin of that story.

Once there was a woman called Boann. She was the daughter of Delbáeth, one of the Tuatha Dé Danann. She lived with her husband Nechtan in the province of Leinster. Boann was strong and stubborn, and didn't like being told what to do. In fact, if you told her not to do something, she would get annoyed, and even do the actual thing you told her not to! Do you know someone like that?

Anyway, not far from Nechtan and Boann's house was a very special place. It was a secret well. This well had (and still has) many different names, but one of them was 'Connla's Well'. It was known to be a place of knowledge and power, and was very much connected to the fairy world.

Surrounding this well were nine magical hazel trees, and each one produced magical hazelnuts. Some of these fell from the trees and into the water, and it is said that some were eaten by a particular salmon, and this salmon possessed great knowledge. But there's more about that in another story!

Boann learned of this well and thought she might like to visit it on her daily walk. But her husband Nechtan didn't approve.

'Wife! Now you keep a distance from that well, do you hear me? There are other places you can take your morning walk.'

'Why husband?' said Boann, frowning. 'Why should I keep clear of it, tell me?'

'It is a magical well,' he said, 'and we can't begin to know its power. I fear for your safety. Don't you go near it!'

'Hmph,' said Boann. 'Well, husband, you may be afraid, but I am not!'

Nothing made Boann more cross than someone telling her what to do. Especially if it was her own husband.

'I'm not afraid of a well!' she thought, and she tossed her head back with pride.

The next day she put on her walking boots and made her way down towards the secret well. It was an enchanting place, and she stopped for a moment to take in her beautiful surroundings.

Boann was a proud and fair woman, and it almost felt like the place itself was admiring her too.

She walked past the trees down to the well. Beside the well, there was an old sign. On that sign there was an arrow pointing to the right. This was painted in green and showed the direction that people were meant to walk around the well. Underneath was another arrow, painted in red, with a big X through it. It was pointing to the left. Underneath was a big red 'NO', and underneath that, just for good measure, the word 'DON'T!' was written.

It was forbidden to walk around the well in this way.

Now, nothing made Boann more cross than someone telling her what to do, even if it was written on a sign.

'I'll walk whichever way I choose!' she said, tilting her head back proudly – and she began to walk around the well in the opposite direction to the green arrow.

Now I should tell you, to walk *tuathail* around the well meant you were challenging the spirit that lived there, and as Boann began to circle it, she could feel the ground rumble underneath her. Boann was a strong woman and was no fool. Her instincts told her that something was wrong.

A voice spoke from within her own heart. 'Boann,' it said, 'turn back…'

At first Boann thought she was imagining it, and she kept walking, walking around the edge of the well. Circling it one time, two times, three times. And the rumbling continued.

Again the voice came from her heart. 'Boann, will you turn back?'

This time she heard something, but she couldn't quite make out the words, so she kept walking, walking around the edge of the well. Circling four times, five times, six times. And the rumbling got louder.

For the third and final time, her own heart spoke to her. 'Boann. Please turn back!'

This time she heard it loud and clear.

But of course, nothing made Boann more cross than someone telling her what to do, even if it was her own heart!

And so she continued on circling the well, now for the seventh time. The rumbling was now a roar. The spirit of the water was summoned, and rose up through the stones and rocks.

As Boann completed her seventh circle, the mighty waters burst forth from the earth, scooped up the proud Boann, and washed her away.

Oh dear.

By walking *tuathail* around the well, Boann had challenged the waters, and they, in turn, had risen to meet her challenge. Despite her stubbornness, though, her heart was pure, and her spirit strong. The waters respected this and do you know what? Her spirit became one with the spirit of the water. The two forces combined became a powerful river, with all the pride and fire of Boann and all the knowledge held in that well.

The river was named after her: Boann, or the River Boyne.

To this day it travels from its source in County Kildare, all the way out to the coast, where it enters the Irish Sea between County Louth and County Meath. It flows for seventy miles; ten miles for each circle of the well that Boann walked, when she summoned the waters forth.

15

THE WHITE TROUT

Once upon a time, in the county of Mayo there was a lovely lady who lived near a lake. She was engaged to marry the king's son when he returned from fighting in a war. Alas, the king's son was lost in battle. Word got back to the lady that this had happened, and although the other warriors never found him, they guessed that his enemies had thrown him into the lake on the other side of the great mountain.

The lady was so sad that she began to fade. Her complexion turned pale, and her hair turned pure white. One day she faded so much that she disappeared completely. Some people said that she had gone to follow the king's son to the otherworld; others said that it was the fairies that had taken her in, to mind her.

Soon after the lady disappeared, a white trout was seen in the lake for the first time. People didn't know what to make of this creature that was pure white. Year after year this white trout was seen swimming in the water, and people believed it to be a magical fish, so they never caught it.

One day some soldiers came to the area near the lake to set up a camp. When they heard the stories about the white trout, they laughed and laughed at the people in the village. They thought it was rubbish that this little fish could be something magical! Not only did they make fun of the fish, but one of the soldiers declared that he was going to catch it, cook it in a frying pan, and eat it for his breakfast!

Sure enough, he caught it, but when he put it in the pan, didn't it let out a noise that sounded so human! He could swear it said 'ouch' in a tiny voice. Instead of taking it off the fire though, he simply turned it over to its other side and ignored the noise. He did this several times, but no matter how often he turned it, there was no sign of the trout cooking in the pan. You see, fish usually cook quickly, and you can see the skin change colour. But if you are not sure if something is cooked or not, one way to test it is to stick a fork in it to see.

The soldier picked up his fork and stuck it into the side of the fish to test it, and didn't he get the fright of his life! The trout leapt out of the frying pan, onto the ground, and immediately turned into a beautiful lady, dressed all in white. On her arm she had a little cut where the soldier had stuck the fork, and it was bleeding.

'You have cut me, you villain!' she said. 'Why did you take me from my lake? I must stay there and look for my beloved in the cool waters.'

The soldier was very frightened and started shaking like a leaf as the lady continued to speak.

'If my true love comes back while I am away from the water and I miss him, the fault will be yours.' She flashed a look of anger at the soldier. 'I will turn you into a little pinkeen and I will hunt you down through the lakes and rivers until the sun sets no more!'

The soldier begged the lady for mercy (for he now realised she was, of course, some kind of magical creature).

'Please pardon me, my lady, and spare my life!' he said, still trembling like a leaf.

'Return me at once to the lake, and I will consider mercy,' she said. 'You must tend the fire by this lake each night and not leave here until my beloved returns. You must renounce your fighting ways and become a simple and good man.'

As soon as these words were spoken, the lady vanished again, and there on the ground was the little white trout, tossing and gasping for water.

The soldier quickly scooped the fish up into his cupped hands. As he did, he noticed the little red mark where he had stuck the fork in its side. He rushed to the lake, and as he released the trout into the water, the whole lake turned blood red and stayed that way for a year and a day.

The soldier kept his promise, and each day went to the edge of the lake where he lit a fire. He would often see the white trout, and she would swim up to him sometimes and stay for a while.

He was no longer a soldier but a keeper of the fire. A good and simple man. He grew very old in years and was respected by the villagers for his kindness.

One day, as he sat tending the fire, the trout swam up to him, and beside her was a second fish, just the same, pure white.

The soldier knew that the trout had finally found her beloved. He knew that because of this he was finally released from his promise and was free to go. By now though, he was a wise hermit and a very old man, so he decided to stay where he was, and tend the fire until the end of his days.

16

GRÁINNE'S HAIR

Gráinne loved playing by the boats. Ever since she could remember, her favourite thing was the smell of the sea, the roar of the waves, and the taste of the salt in the air near her home.

Her father, Eoghan, often let her play alongside his ship. She would climb over the boxes of supplies that were waiting to be loaded. You'd often find her swinging through the air from the thick wet ropes that tied the ship to the dock. Her long red hair would blow in the wind as she leaned her head back and laughed with delight.

Sometimes she would sneak on board the ship when nobody was looking. She would pretend she was a sailor, or even a captain, leading her ships off on a great adventure. She had to be careful nobody saw her though, or she would get into trouble!

Her mother, Maeve, you see, was none too fond of Gráinne playing on the ships. 'That's no place for a young girl,' she'd say. 'Whoever heard of a girl being a sailor?'

In those days, you see, it was almost unheard of for a girl to want such things.

How silly!

But this didn't stop Gráinne. In fact, the older she got, the stronger her love for the sea grew, and she wanted nothing more than to sail off on the open waves. Over the years, she'd ask her father if he would take her with him on one of his voyages, but he would simply reply, 'Gráinne, *a stór*, you are too young to come with me.'

Time passed and Gráinne grew older.

A week came when Gráinne's father was about to set sail on a trip to Spain and Gráinne reeeeeeaaaaallllly wanted to go with him this time. The week before, some lads the very same age as her had gone off as cabin boys on a ship. Surely she too was old enough, she thought? So she decided to ask her father once more if she could go with him.

'Oh Gráinne,' said her father, looking down at his shoes. 'You're too—'

Gráinne interrupted him. 'Daddy, don't say I'm too young. I'm as old as many a cabin boy!'

Gráinne's mother, Maeve, was standing nearby. She had a big frown on her face.

'Oh, please let me go with you, Daddy,' said Gráinne. 'I AM old enough, there is no reason for me not to go!'

Eoghan glanced over at his wife. She threw him a glare and shook her head. He turned back to his daughter.

'No, Gráinne, I'm sorry. You can't come with me this time. Perhaps… emm… you are old enough, but… emm… it's your hair!'

'What?' said Gráinne.

'It's your hair. Emm… your lovely long red hair,' said Eoghan. 'It would get tangled up in the rigging ropes when we are out at sea and it would be too dangerous. No, you must stay here safe at home.'

Maeve smiled a smile of relief at her husband, but of course Gráinne was very upset. Her mother tried to put her arm around her to console her but she stormed off to her house.

Back in her bedroom, she sat there with her head in her hands.

'This is so unfair,' she thought. 'That my own hair should stop me sailing on the seven seas.'

She looked up and caught a glimpse of her reflection in the mirror. She looked at her long curly red hair flowing down around her shoulders. A smile slowly appeared on her face. A sneaky smile! She had an idea!

The next morning, Eoghan and his crew were about set sail for Spain. Maeve was down at the dock to say goodbye to her husband, and wish him well on his journey. But there was no sign of Gráinne.

'I hope she's not too upset at me,' thought Eoghan, and he was sad that his daughter hadn't come to wave goodbye like she always did.

They were loading the last of the supplies onboard when Eoghan spotted a small

hooded figure boarding the ship. He was
the same size as the cabin boys, but Eoghan
did not recognise him. Eoghan reached over,
pulled back the hood from the small figure
and gasped.

'Gráinne?' he said.

Maeve saw this happen, and also let out a gasp, as she put her two hands to her face in shock. For there in front of her was her daughter Gráinne, and all her lovely hair cut off. She had been trying to disguise herself as one of the cabin boys and sneak onboard!

'Yes, it is me,' said Gráinne, and she pulled out her long locks of red hair from her pocket and handed them to her mother.

'Now, father,' she said, 'my hair will not catch in the ropes, for it will be here, safe at home with my mother!'

Eoghan looked at his daughter, standing there, her hair so short that she was nearly as bald as an egg! A smile grew on his face. He couldn't help but be proud of his daughter's determination.

'Very well, daughter,' he said. 'You have proved that your will is strong! You may sail with me to Spain!'

Gráinne was delighted, but when she looked over she noticed the sadness on her mother's face.

'Don't worry, Mama, I will be fine!' she said, as she hugged her mother tightly. 'My hair will grow back even redder and even stronger. I will return to you safe and sound, and the day will soon come that you will be so proud to call me your daughter.'

And do you know what? All that was true.

Gráinne went off sailing to Spain with her father, and they did return safe and sound.

That journey was only the start of her adventures. She went on many more voyages to distant lands. She became a great sailor, and in time she had a ship of her own to sail, and she commanded many sailors like her father had before her.

She was known by many different names: 'Gráinne Ní Mháille', 'Grace O'Malley' and even 'the Pirate Queen'!

To many, though, she will be remembered by another name. A nickname. It came from that day all those years ago when she chopped off her hair so she could sail to Spain. The name is 'Granuaile' or 'Gráinne Mhaol' – which of course means 'Bald Gráinne'!

17

THE GIANTS' WELL

There's a song that begins with the line 'In Oranmore, in the County Galway'. This story is not the same as the song. It begins in a similar way, true enough, but is a very different tale.

In Oranmore in the County Galway, there is a place called Frenchfort. In Frenchfort, there is a little *boreen* with hedges on either side of it. There are an unusual amount of birds living in these hedges, and they sing very sweetly and loudly – most of the time.

At the end of this boreen there is a well. Local people talk about the well, and one thing they say is that it was not built by human hands…

A long time ago, near the well, there lived two giants. Their names have long been forgotten, or perhaps it was forbidden to speak them, as giants are magical creatures and often feared by people. So, for this story, I will call them Big She and Big He.

Big He and Big She grew up near each other (this was both unusual and fortunate, as there were not many giants in their area). As time passed, they fell very much in love, and the day came where Big He asked Big She to marry him. Of course, she said yes and was delighted with her lovely big husband.

The two of them settled in a (big) little cottage and were very happy together, doing big things and little things around the house and the garden and the village. Both of them liked to help people and would do things like lift big rocks, if a neighbour needed a field cleared (as they had big hands), or they'd help fix the roof on a cottage (because they were very tall), or they'd even defend the village against enemies (as they were very strong).

One day, Big He was called away to help another giant in a battle. It would be a long journey to this battle, even for a giant. Someone needed to tend the crops and the animals, so Big She stayed at home, and set about doing all the normal big things and little things on her own.

After the battle was over, Big He spent some time on the open road, travelling from village to village and meeting new people and helping them. He had never had adventures as a boy.

'I think this lifestyle suits me better!' he thought. 'I don't want to be tied down in a little village with animals and crops and doing the same thing every day. I'm going to have a big adventure. Big She has all she needs at home and will be fine there by herself!'

Now meanwhile, back in Frenchfort, Big She was patiently waiting for her husband. She was the one who had to stay and tend the animals and crops, remember? Each day she would look out the window of their (big) little cottage, hoping to see him pounding up the boreen. But each day the boreen was empty of her husband's footsteps. His journey would take time, yes, but when the days stretched into weeks, and weeks into months, she knew something was very wrong. She feared that Big He had been injured in the battle, or maybe worse.

It was nearly a year after Big He had left home, when a travelling merchant came through Frenchfort. He met Big She, and of course, seeing that she was a giant, he struck up a conversation.

'You're the second giant I've seen this year!' he remarked.

Big She's eyes lit up when she heard this news. Could the other giant be her husband? Could it be Big He? She asked the merchant to describe the fellow.

'He was big!' said the merchant.

'We are all big, sure aren't we giants!' Big She rolled her eyes in frustration. 'Tell me more about him – his appearance, his clothes…

The merchant described the giant he had seen. Long black hair. Yes. Green eyes. Yes. Red boots. Yes. And a jacket with bird sewn into the pocket.

Big She let out an excited gasp, 'It's him! It's him!'

Before he'd left for the battle, Big She he had sewn a little blackbird into Big He's jacket pocket, to remind him of the hedges of Frenchfort. To remind him of his home. She asked the merchant for every little detail. Was he all right? Yes. Was he hurt? No. Had he lost his memory – for surely this was the only reason he hadn't returned home to Frenchfort?

The merchant had to tell Big She the truth. He told her how he'd shared a mug of ale with the giant in a tavern. He told her how Big He had talked about his NEW life

of adventure. He hadn't mentioned a thing about Frenchfort, nor that he had a wife!

It was then that poor Big She began to cry. Why wasn't Big He coming home? The more she thought about Big He, the more Big She cried.

Now she was a giant, remember, and each tear she shed was as big as a bucket. They trickled down her cheek like small rivers.

She cried so much that these rivers flowed down onto the ground and the waters began to rise.

She cried so much that the merchant and the villagers ran to climb the trees as they thought they would surely drown.

She cried so much that the birds in the hedges stopped singing, her sadness was so great.

Just when everyone thought she would flood the whole village with her tears, she took off her wedding ring and threw it to the ground. She flung it with such force that it made a huge hole where it landed, and all her tears began to flow down into it, making a giant whirlpool.

When she stopped crying, what was left was a very deep well full of giant's tears.

Meanwhile, many miles away, Big He woke up in a hay barn with a sore head. He would often wake up with a sore head and a cold body, as this life of adventure was not all it was cracked up to be. He had been using his jacket for a pillow, and when he rolled over this particular morning, his eyes fell upon the bird sewn into the jacket pocket.

Not only did his head feel sore, but his heart did too. He missed dear wife, Big She.

'How selfish I have been,' he thought.

After a year of adventures and wandering from town to town, he realised that his days were empty without her by his side. He picked himself up and headed home, across fields and mountains and lakes, back towards Frenchfort, back to beg Big She's forgiveness.

When he arrived at Frenchfort, he noticed how quiet it was. He noticed that all the birds had stopped singing.

His wife opened the door of the cottage, and this time it was Big He who burst into tears.

'Please forgive me, my darling,' he said. 'I wanted a life of adventure, it is true. But it was empty without you – I have finally come to my senses!'

Now Big She was very angry – too angry forgive him. That night Big He had to sleep in the (small) shed of the (big) little cottage. In fact, for a month he slept in that shed, each night going to sleep with a jacket for a pillow and straw for a blanket.

Each night he would look at the little bird on his jacket, and hope that the next day would be different.

Each morning he got up and picked hundreds of flowers and put them by the door of the cottage for Big She.

Each morning he made a delicious breakfast of porridge and honey and put it at the door of the cottage for Big She.

Each morning he wrote poems for her too and laid them on the doorstep. Poems telling her how selfish he had been, poems about how much she loved her, and poems begging her forgiveness.

Finally, after a month of flowers and poems and porridge, Big She opened the door and spoke to her husband.

'Now it is my turn to go on an adventure,' she said.

Big He looked very sad. 'You are leaving me?' he said. 'I suppose that is exactly what I deserve.'

But Big She turned to him and gave him a wink. 'I suppose you can come too,' she said. 'As long as you keep writing poems for me and making me breakfast.'

Big He reached out to Big She and gave her the biggest hug Frenchfort had ever seen!

In that moment, as the two giants stood there in their embrace, the birds in the trees started singing again.

The next morning Big She and Big He left their animals and house in the charge of their neighbours, and set off on their adventures together. They would travel the land, helping people, where the help of giants was needed, but this time they would do it together.

Just as they were leaving the village Big He remembered the wedding ring. 'Shall I

dive down into the well and fetch it for you?'
he said.

'No, husband,' said Big She. 'I will leave
it where it is, for it only reminds me of my
tears. You can buy me another one on our
travels.' And with that, the two giants left,
and never returned.

You can still find their well though, in
Frenchfort. It is down that little boreen,
hidden behind some bushes. The locals will
tell you that on a quiet day, if you drink from
that well, the water is salty, and can fill you
with sadness.

But if you drink from the well on a day
when the birds are singing loudly, then the
water is sweet, and your years will be filled
with happiness and adventure.

NOTES

Thanks for reading this book! Here are a few notes and facts that you might find interesting. They are in no particular order, just some things I thought about while writing the stories.

From **Fionn and the Salmon**: Fionn Mac Cumhaill is spelled a bunch of different ways. You may sometimes even hear him called 'Finn Mc Cool'.

From **What a Big Baby**: The Giant's Boot is part of the Giant's Causeway in County Antrim. If you walk down a little path to the sea at Port Noffer, you will find the boot!

A *doteen* is a word we use a lot to describe someone sweet or adorable. A *dote* can be used too, and the '*een*' usually means someone smaller.

From **The King's Ears**: Lough Oighinn / Lough Íne / Lough Hyne is in County Cork and is spelled a bunch of different ways! There is still a castle in the middle of the lake and if you listen carefully you might hear uilleann pipes being played nearby. Uilleann pipes are a musical instrument that has a bag, bellows, drones, and a chanter. You use your elbow to pump up the bag with the bellows, and then you play the chanter with your fingers, and the notes are made there and by the drone(s).

From **Cake**: Blackrock Tower was built in 1954. It is located at the end of the Salthill Promenade (also called 'the Prom') At the time of me writing this, it is painted yellow. People gather here all year round to swim every day, and in summer hundreds of people jump off it into the sea. Many say 'Wheeeee!' as they jump.

From **The Fairy Ship of Roses**: Would you like to learn to sing the song from this story? I have put a link to it on my website, so you can listen to an example of it, and even find the chords to play on the guitar if you like. You will find a link on www.orlamcgovern.com

From **Black and White**: When I was writing this book, my friend Bekka reminded me of a song I love called 'Orca Killer Whale'. It was written by a songwriter called John Spillane – I really like his songs. The song is about the day the whales swam up the River Lee, too, on 16 July 2001!

From **Seven Times Round**: *Tuathail* means anti-clockwise. There is also an old word for it used in English too called widdershins.

Connla's Well is sometimes called Conla's Well. There is another story naming Conla's Well as the origin of the River Shannon. Wow! Connla's Well was very busy it seems!

From **Gráinne's Hair**: *a stór* means dear, or dearest, in Irish.

From **The Giants' Well**: A boreen is a little road. *Bóthar* means road in Irish (*Gaeilge*) and 'een' at the end makes it a little road!

'In Oranmore, in the County Galway' is the first line of a traditional folk song called 'The Galway Shawl'. The first record of it being collected was by Sam Henry from the singing of Bridget Kealey in Dungiven. You can look up many different versions of it these days, with different people singing it.

STORYTELLERS of Ireland

AOS SCÉAL ÉIREANN

www.storytellersofireland.org

Ireland is famed throughout the world for the art of storytelling. The seancaithe and scéalaí, the tradition bearers and storytellers passed the old stories down through the generations. Today, in the 21st century, there has been a revivial od the ancient art founded in 2003, Storytellers of Ireland / Aos Scéal Éireann is an all-Ireland voluntary organisation with charitable status.

Our aim is to promote the practice, study and knowledge of oral storytelling in Ireland through the preservation and perpetuation of traditional storytelling and the development of storytelling as a contemporary art. We aim to foster storytelling skills among all age groups, from all cultural backgrounds. We also aim to explore new contexts for storytelling in public places – in schools, community centres and libraries, in care centres and prisons, in theatres, arts centres and at festivals throughout the entire island of Ireland.

Storytelling is an intimate and interactive art. A storyteller tells from memory rather than reading from a book. A tale is not just the spoken equivalent of a literary short story. It has no set text, but is endlessly re-created in the telling. The listener is an essential part of the storytelling process. For stories to live, they need the hearts, minds and ears of listeners. Without the listener there is no story.

Le fiche bliain anuas, tá borradh agus fás tagaithe ar shean-ghairm inste scéal. Tá clú agus cáil ar na scéalta ársa agus ar an seanchas atá le fáil i nÉirinn. Le déanaí tá siad arís i mbéal an phobail, idir óg is sean, is i ngach áird is aicme.